The BLESSED CURSE

DINESH .N. VERMA

INDIA • SINGAPORE • MALAYSIA

Copyright © Dinesh .N. Verma 2024
All Rights Reserved.

ISBN 979-8-89363-988-9

This book has been published with all efforts taken to make the material error-free after the consent of the author. However, the author and the publisher do not assume and hereby disclaim any liability to any party for any loss, damage, or disruption caused by errors or omissions, whether such errors or omissions result from negligence, accident, or any other cause.

While every effort has been made to avoid any mistake or omission, this publication is being sold on the condition and understanding that neither the author nor the publishers or printers would be liable in any manner to any person by reason of any mistake or omission in this publication or for any action taken or omitted to be taken or advice rendered or accepted on the basis of this work. For any defect in printing or binding the publishers will be liable only to replace the defective copy by another copy of this work then available.

The novel is entirely a work of fiction. The names, characters and incidents portrayed are the product of author's imagination. Any resemblance to any person, living or dead, events and locations is entirely coincidental. While every care has been taken not to hurt anybody's sentiments, the writer owes unqualified apologies if inadvertently hurt is caused to anyone.

Disclaimer:

All rights reserved. No part of this book may be reproduced or transmitted in any form or by any means, electronic or mechanical, including photocopying, recording, or by any information storage and retrieval system without the written permission of the writer or his authorized agency.

Writer's details:

E.mail: dineshnarain.verma@gmail.com
Blog: khushdilverma.blogspot.com
Mobile no. 9818089504

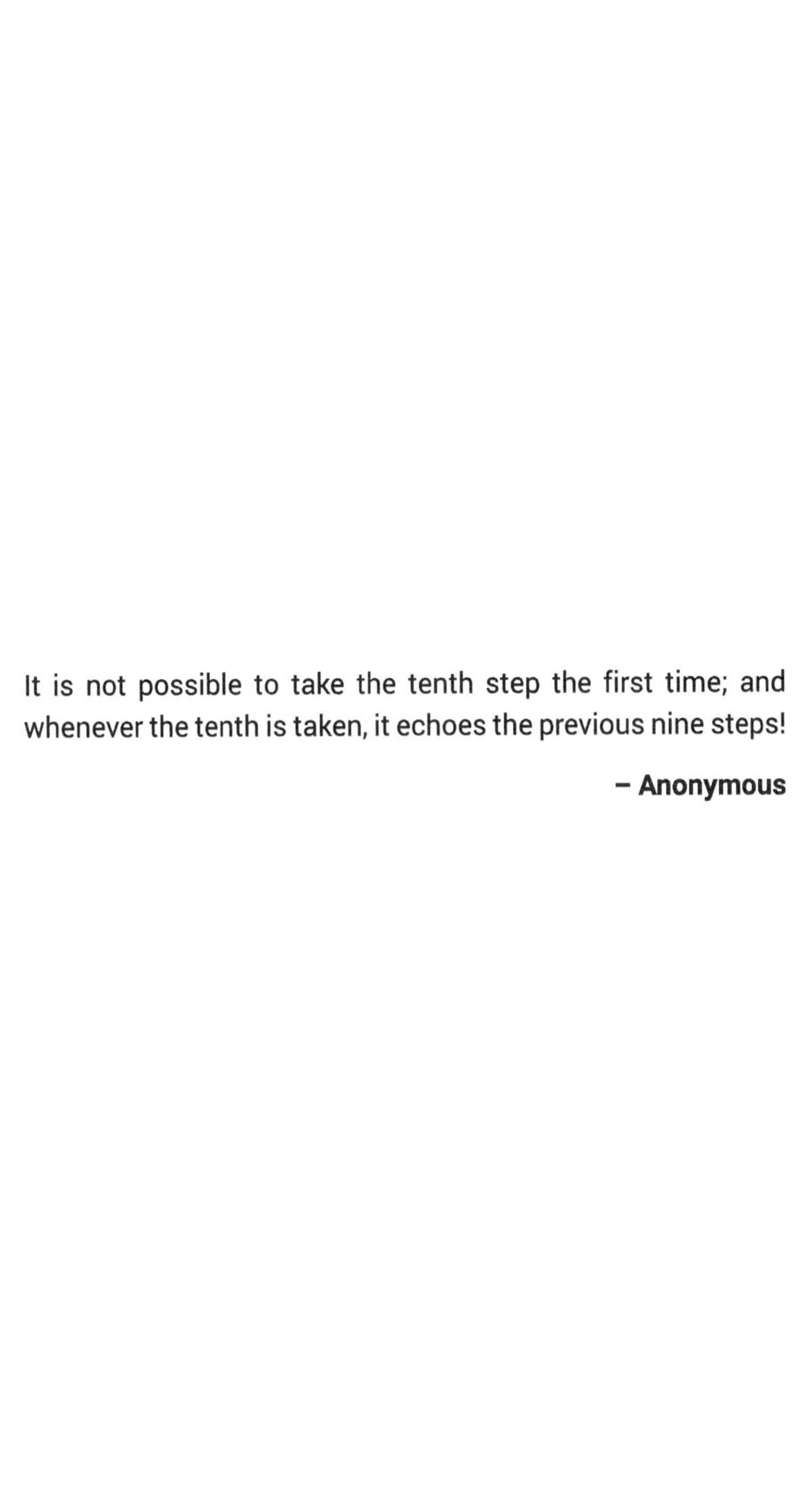

It is not possible to take the tenth step the first time; and whenever the tenth is taken, it echoes the previous nine steps!

– Anonymous

CONTENTS

FOREWORD

India emerged into shimmering light of freedom from a long and dark tunnel of slavery in 1947 and, thanks to its giant leaders then, it moved ahead with vision and determination to usher in an era of peace, plenty and prosperity. In a span of seven decades since then, three generations have treaded on the surface of the country beginning with the one that existed around the period when India was struggling to wrestle out freedom from the colonial yoke and continued further as part of the nation on the move to the present generation of young girls and boys who are grappling to create space for themselves in a highly competitive world. Caught in the middle are those belonging to my generation who, on the one hand, try to match their steps with strides of their growing children in order to keep pace with fast changing world and, on the other, keep looking back over the shoulder to foster the legacy of their fore-parents.

Standing now at the edge of seventh decade, can anyone from present generation, even with divine gift of fertile imagination, visualize the wretched conditions that prevailed during the period around Independence when their fore-parents lived? Can anyone imagine the extent of scarcity and paucity of resources at that point of time? Can anyone measure level of plight and intensity of pain that our predecessors had to bear? Can anyone of this generation, at this stage, imagine the pathetic state of our country which was cast asunder after massive tragedy of partition involving mass migration that rendered millions of families homeless and rootless? Do they have any idea about the amount of struggle that went into rehabilitating the uprooted millions?

We can, at best, endeavour to be empathetic imagining the plight of our predecessors during those challenging days, but would definitely fail to feel the reality of harsh truth of their day to day living unless there is someone belonging to that period to tell us, albeit with a touch of emotions based on their personal experiences, how they lived during those times, someone who can make us feel as if those who lived and suffered then are even now holding our hands, someone who can help us in creating a lasting emotional bond between them and us. And that is what precisely the author, through his book 'The Blessed Curse', has attempted to do.

Mr. Dinesh .N. Verma, an accomplished author, whom I have known for decades, was born in the decade that was filled with hectic political activity which culminated into attainment of freedom and since then he grew in years moving alongside the advancing steps of the nation, watching with curious eyes changing face of the country from rough and rugged then to beautiful and magnificent now. Bestowed with the gift of blessed curse of nostalgia, the author, through the pages of this book, has attempted to describe the facets of transformation that took place in the country punctuated with good to read anecdotes and episodes in simple and lucid language. Having gone through the manuscript I can assure that it is fun and pleasure for people of all ages to read this book. We are, indeed, blessed to have Mr. Verma with us to give us a peek into the times that have brought us to present era where India, as a nation and the society at large, is raring to take up the coming challenges with vision and confidence. My sincere appreciation and kudos for an interesting take on the phenomenon of change in the country during the past seven decades.

– Sanjay Raizada
CEO, Taal Systems Pvt Ltd

PREFACE

Of all the maladies that overtake an ageing person, 'Nostalgic Attack' is the one which is quite common and is naturally taken as an inevitable curse to be borne with gift of utmost rectitude. But it seems equally true that since it comes to a person as a blessing in disguise, it deserves to be treated as 'The Blessed Curse'.

Nostalgia is a wistful memory of past incidents and discourses which come back flashing in fits and starts to persons of advanced age. They do not have much to look forward but enough to look back frequently to pick even trivial incidents to brood over with comparisons based on their perceptions of the past and the present. It becomes a curse when an unpleasant incident that took place in the past comes up to haunt him. But if pleasant happenings or sweet words spoken in the past take hold of his mind, they serve him as a soothing balm.

Nostalgic incidents bring both tears and cheers depending upon the profile of the nostalgic person. Going by the old adage that 'to think of pleasure is also pleasure' thoughts of pleasant moments of past naturally turn up to a nostalgic person with a sense of greater pleasure than the actual occurrences of those pleasurable moments.

When young, one tastes the sweetness of honey from the packed bottles, but on becoming old he has to extract it from the beehive of life. For those who are able to do it successfully, it becomes 'blessing' as the nostalgia in that case helps to wipe out the hurt and the pain caused by tragic incidents of the past or the impact of unflattering words during the years gone by.

This apart, the people of advancing age with nostalgic tendencies are asset to society when they share with their youngsters their experiences linking present with their childhood days, marked with sharp contrasts and deep socio-economic ramifications. Their penchant to narrate their ways and styles of living, bitter and sweet incidents that they encountered becomes a valuable source of understanding the past and every word spoken by them adds up to the precious treasure for the posterity. Their nostalgia, in that case, becomes a natural bridge connecting the two distant ends of time, thereby linking the present with the past as it evolved over decades since the attainment of Independence. Nostalgia of such elderly people becomes a viable medium for the present crop of youths for acquiring firsthand knowledge about them and their times, their styles of living, their wants and cravings, their culture and customs, their faith and beliefs, their shortcomings, their struggles and achievements. They are the precious link between the decades rolled by, carving bit by bit the shape of things then, now and, of course, the future ahead, which will need to be moulded neatly from the present with strong thread of continuity of healthy traditions, values and well laid cultural ethos.

It is of tremendous importance that growing children of today know all about their fore-parents. But relevant information about them should not be thrust into their brains as a dry stuff of history, but through their active involvement in talks punctuated with interesting tales and anecdotes. Spread over preceding seven decades are broadly three generations and the new crop needs to be literally transformed into living with their fore-parents holding their hands.

It is difficult to place this book into any specific literary category. But it certainly is not the history. Though written with an eye on coming generations, it, nevertheless, should make an interesting read for persons of all ages, provided youths are not biased against all that is old, and the ageing lot is not averse to all that is modern.

– Dinesh .N. Verma 'Khushdil'

PROLOGUE

It is through a compact group of a family with three generations merging frequently on domestic forum as well as on the occasions of family functions with large gatherings of vocal lots that effort has been made to link the present with the past through preceding seven decades.

Here is a large family of the grand old man, Jagdamba Prasad, his brothers and sisters, sons and daughters, nephews and nieces, grandchildren and a long trail of his old and new friends.

Grand Old Man, Jagdamba Prasad & His Spouse, Pushpa Devi

The grand old man is a character named Jagdamba Prasad, popularly known as Jagan Babu, who suffers from frequent bouts of nostalgia. Tall and lanky, every wrinkle of his wheatish face reveals toughness of journey that life has been for him. He was born at a time when India shook off the colonial yoke and moved to breathe fresh air of freedom. And, since then, he has been a curious witness to fast changing contours of our socio–economic and political landscape.

He is the one who keeps blowing hot and cold when flashes of past and buffets of present strike him off and on. He feels strongly that though the country rotted like a stagnant pool by the dirt of slavery for years, it was, nevertheless, wrapped in a strong social fabric, well-knit with the threads of soft emotions of humanism. And naturally he is now over awed by tidal waves of changes which, he feels, are threatening to gradually sweep away traditionally nurtured edifice of our social structure despite its strong base.

He lives now with the blessed curse that comes alive before his eyes, in fits and starts, like dreams alternated with flashes of weird phantoms conjured by things not to his liking and colourful images triggered by things of his choice.

Jagan Babu is accustomed to spending most of his time either in his study room or on a long comfortable armed chair near huge oval dining table that lay in the drawing -cum-dining hall adjacent to the kitchen of the flat of his son, Ravindra Kumar, in one of the colonies in East Delhi. He enjoys reading his newspaper while sipping early morning tea as the rising sun throws its soothing bright rays through the glass panes. Interestingly, the dining table has assumed symbolic significance as it represents three generations of India when members of his family gather there twice a day, on breakfast and dinner almost daily and on holidays on lunch as well unless there is programme to go out. They usually begin with natural conversation and soon warm up to lively discussions on subjects ranging from political landscape of the country to latest films released. The arguments are naturally loud and noisy as each one of them has been looking at life through the lenses of their own colours as they grew from year to year.

Jagan Babu sits at one end of the table and on his left sits the grand old lady, his wife, Pushpa Devi. She too, like her husband, suffers from the same common old age disease except that while Pushpa Devi's flashes of the past remain confined to family incidents to 'who said what', Jagan Babu's nostalgia strays wildly to touch upon almost everything under the sun.

Jagan Babu, like those of his age, was a toddler on the eve of Independence in1947 and, since then has been witness to phenomenon of changing India from languishing state to what it is now after seven decades. He has practically grown with the country.

He was there when the new India was yet to be born, with all the pangs associated with the birth of a sovereign nation. He saw it coming to life in the midnight of August 15,1947, watched it from the cradle and then as a boy and man, and now, as an ageing person, seeing it running at the pace of marathon, carrying on its shoulder the baggage of the past, a mixed bag of good and bad in equal measure. He had seen as a child the naked dance of madness and blood curdling communal frenzy associated with the partition of the country in 1947, And now while he feels proud as an Indian at the marvellous feats of achievement that have changed the face of the country from rugged to glamourous, watches also with shock and concern growing madness on roads, automobiles and public property being burnt on slightest provocations, Indians killing Indians on flimsy grounds like four yards of parking space in a residential colony. Nurtured since his childhood on the adage 'Love thy neighbour', he now sees with tearful eyes "Hit thy neighbour" syndrome gaining ground.

He is at times baffled to find India completely transformed into an identity which is quite alien to what he knew as a child and a boy and even as a man and, ironically, which is not entirely the one he and his peers had wished it to be, with all the apparent glamour. And he loses no opportunity to say it aloud to provoke many to disagree more than to agree with him. And why not? After all, the vast Indian landscape is being seen by three existing generations through three different sets of binoculars.

It is not that people of Jagan Babu's age are blind to the giant strides that the country has made to emerge as a vibrant economic power from the stagnant pool that it was at the time of partition of the country. But many amongst the thinking lot feel strongly that the process of transformation from traditional to modern has been taking its toll to an extent that we cannot be sure of the shape that India will take ultimately with the passage of time. The ghastliness of terrifying incidents reported in newspapers and viewed on the small screen, day in and day out, throws them in dilemma which they find difficult to ignore.

They are the ones who recall frequently fond memories of their childhood days. Those were the days when the concept of residential colonies was alien to them. They lived in what was called mohallas. Those were the days when large middle-class families lived together as joint families in traditionally built houses with total obliteration of lines of distinction between a real and a cousin.

Jagan Babu is one of those ageing people who are blessed with the talent to convert even the curse into a blessing. It is not that nostalgia does not turn up as memory of the unpleasant happenings from the past to haunt him. But he is able to locate moments of happiness from the debris of the past and live on them despite everything having unrecognizably changed in preceding seven decades.

★ ★ ★

Jagdamba Prasad's Son, Ravindra Kumar & Son's Spouse, Ratna

And then come in descending order, Jagdamba Prasad's son, Ravindra and his spouse Ratna, sitting at the other end of the table. He is the bread winner of the family, representing the generation which is sandwiched between the old conservatives and the ultra-modern. They are the ones who look forward endeavouring to match their steps with those of their growing children in order to keep pace with fast changing world, holding smart phones in their hands and laptops on their laps. And, at the same time, they look back to the past, with deep rooted traditions and well-established values as inherited from the previous generation. It is as if they are, all the time, trying to balance the present with the past as well as with the future. And, in the process, many amongst them are caught in whirlpool of contradictions and make a mess of their lives in a bid to resolve conflicting situations thrown up by the mix of past and present with aspirations for future.

And in their endeavour to combine the threads of past with present and with aspirations for future, they are forced to join mad race for acquiring material gains to sustain their lives and survive in a highly competitive world with semblance of dignity, provide adequate education to their children, settle them with life of their own, and at the same time, take care of their ageing parents, keep them happy by maintaining pleasant relations with all those who matter to them. And they have to do it all within their limited resources. No wonder some amongst the people of their generation go off the track to amass wealth, flouting ethical norms with impunity, pushing their families to live luxuriously. While some people around watch them with contempt, there are lots of people who look at them enviously for their luxurious ways of living. And those who are able to withstand the compulsions of over commercialization, without their integrity tampered by day-to-day pressures, have to live all the time in struggling mode. The clan of such people is gradually shrinking, but it is they who endeavour to help society to sustain itself with dignity.

Jagdamba Prasad's Grandchildren: Rakhi, Rohan and Pinki

On the middle chairs of the dining table sit fond grandchildren of Jagdamba Prasad. He forgets his age when in their company and becomes their friend, sharing with them his pains and pleasures at things around the world. Ironically, they are the ones who come on the wrong side of Jagdamba Prasad more often with their provocative remarks and behaviour which leave him writhing in genuine or mock anger at things not palatable to him in the modern-day India. And naturally so, as all the three, being in the age group of fifteen to twenty five, find in their hands, instead of the chalk and slate which Jagan Babu held in his tiny hands, the iPad, laptop and smart phone, to play and fiddle with for hours, carrying tons of weight of books on their shoulders to learn everything to compete in this age of cut throat competition and to join the mad race to build their careers as they grow. Rakhi, who is in her twenty fifth year, is sensible and mature, Rohan, twenty-one, is carefree and casual and Pinki, in her eighteenth year, is cute and curious. They are at times argumentative to the extent of being irritating to their grandfather and to their parents, but their queries are seldom brushed aside by their grandfather.

They do grow but they come at an edge where they have to forget to grow on valued tracks of life. They are what the parents are making them, and society is offering them to be. They are from the generation which is sharply divided between the most brilliant and the pathetically good for nothing. And in between are juxtaposed the mediocre struggling to survive in the midst of competition with the brilliant lot.

★ ★ ★

****

Through Jagan Babu's nostalgic flashes, his incessant narrations to meet persistent probing questions by his curious grandchildren, sporadic discussions and arguments during gatherings of relations and friends on varied occasions, it is endeavoured by the author to unfold the 'Years in Reverse' upon varied aspect of life as lived, seen and absorbed by him since his childhood.

****

THE GET-TOGETHER

After confirmed reservation in Rajdhani for Mumbai was in hand, there was lot of excitement, as the entire family looked forward to spending fun time there after a very long time. Ravindra and Ratna got hectically busy in making arrangements for family's participation in the marriage of Shandilya's granddaughter. Shandilya was Jagan Babu's old colleague and a close friend. During their service period, families of both lived in proximity in Mumbai, which was then called Bombay and, naturally, developed close relationship.

Since the family was already committed to spend the coming Sunday evening at Shamsher Singh's residence at Rama Krishna Puram, where Alekh Sharma and Mahesh Goyal would also be joining them with their families, it was decided to utilize day time for shopping at Saket mall. Shamsher, Alekh and Mahesh were old colleagues and close friends of Jagan Babu. Accordingly, on Sunday, after Ratna with Pushpa Devi had left by cab for Rama Krishna Puram, Jagan Babu, Rakhi, Rohan, and Pinky accompanied Ravindra for Saket in his car.

It was smooth run on the Ring Road until the car entered Lajpat Nagar flyover where it had to stop abruptly to join a long trail of stranded vehicles. Vehicle after vehicle kept adding up and there seemed no easy way out of long jam. There had occurred a serious incidence of road rage at the end of the flyover.

After about an hour of restless wait, the car moved in slow motion and crossed the flyover, virtually crawling at chicken neck at the end of the flyover, where a dead body lay covered with cloth, and police was working to clear the mess.

Their minds clouded with the sight of tragic incident on road, Jagan Babu and others in the car kept sitting silent all through the drive till they reached Saket. Once inside the mall, they looked for a cosy corner, away from the madding crowd, for Jagan Babu to be seated comfortably as he habitually avoided spending long hours at market places. While others got busy in shopping, Jagan Babu settled on a cushioned sofa, snatched the magazine from his bag and began to shuffle its pages. But, his mind being still obsessed with tragic site of accident, he could not concentrate and put the magazine aside. He sat with his eyes closed with thoughtful concern for the people at large.

Accidents understandable, but increasing incidents of road rage crimes, very unfortunate! The entire country seems to be on short fuse, all pervading story of growing intolerance and increasing impatience. Road rage cases are being reported in newspapers every now and then. Recently a 61-yr-old man was dragged out of his car by men on motorbike who punched him severely for not giving pass on a Delhi road which was clearly clogged with heavy traffic. He would have been shot dead if he had failed to keep his cool and not handled the aggressive lot with patience and tact.

Ravindra and Rakhi came there to persuade him to select clothes of his choice but found Jagan Babu lost in thoughts. They decided not to disturb him.

Unmindful of visit of Ravindra and Rakhi, Jagan Babu's mind, in the meantime, had been dragged by the past when, instead of expected mob thrashing, he with his friend came out gloriously from an adverse situation on the dint of their cool-headed approach.

He once accompanied his friend Alekh who was on his way in his jeep to attend some official work. As the jeep was passing through the road adjacent to the gates of Aligarh University, a group of teenaged boys came out running abruptly from the inner lane to catch a low flying severed kite and the first boy, who emerged on the road, was hit by the bumper of the jeep. Blood oozed out of his forehead. The driver wanted to keep going for fear of being thrashed, but he had to stop when rebuffed by Alekh. They both jumped from the jeep and rushed towards the injured boy. Alekh picked him up seeking help, at the same time, from the students standing at a distance in groups. As against their fear that they would be hauled up by them, couple of them came fast and sat down with them at the rear of the jeep and were helpful in handling the injured boy who was crying out of pain. They rushed to Emergency of the Aligarh Medical college and handed over the boy in the care of the doctor. In the meantime, quite a crowd of students gathered at the lobby. At Alekh's behest the parents of the injured boy were informed. The doctor, who attended the boy, came out after some time and announced that necessary treatment had been given and the boy was alright as injury was not serious at all. As soon as the doctor went in, parents of the patient were seen landing at the foyer baffled and bewildered. It was a pleasant shock to both of them when students diverted the couple towards them telling them to 'go and thank them who saved your son'. The parent rushed towards them and virtually fell on their feet. Alekh and he stood like statues surprised at the unexpected soft and sweet behaviour of the students towards them. After speaking reassuring words to the parent and thanking the gathering for their cooperation, they came home relaxed but not before filing report at the police station to avoid any future problem.

At around four, Ravindra and Rakhi came there and found him this time alert and waiting for them. He was persuaded to move to a shopping outfit where he was pressed hard to purchase a shirt and a pant despite resistance by him on the ground that he had enough of everything for himself.

★ ★ ★

By about five in the evening, they completed their purchasing to the extent they could do without Ratna's marketing support and proceeded towards Shamsher Singh's flat. Shamsher Singh, Alekh Sharma and Mahesh Goyal were chatting at the gate when they reached the flat, and except Jagan Babu, who stayed out to join his friends, and Ravindra, who was parking the vehicle, all others went in and virtually fell down on sofa in the drawing room. After some time, Shamsher Singh, accompanied by his friends and Ravindra, entered the drawing room gossiping in their typical styles.

Sensing from pulled down faces of Rakhi, Rohan, and Pinky that something was wrong, Shamsher Singh asked Jagan Babu, "What happened? All of you look crestfallen. What is it?"

"Yes, I also found them low. I thought they are tired," added Goyal.

"It is nothing," Jagan Babu explained the reason. "While proceeding towards Saket, we were stuck up in traffic jam on Lajpat Nagar flyover because of road rage with a fatal casualty. Police was doing its job when our car passed through that tragic spot. The sight of that tragic scene dampened our spirits."

"I find that most of the fights are happening on roads and the reason is that traffic on the roads is becoming quite unmanageable," said Shamsher Singh.

"Yes, you will find the scene quite disturbing if you watch the traffic movement on Delhi roads from a vantage point," commented Alekh. "Apart from haphazard processions of hopping pedestrians, you will see moving vehicles of all shapes and size, from imported big cars to rugged buses swarming the roads, like a huge multitude of fish swimming through overflowing river, rubbing bodies to overtake others on slow moving traffic. Motorbikes, which have practically replaced bicycles, run parallel to cars, buses and trucks, their riders displaying their skills in acrobatics, with jumps and dives through the narrow spaces between the two speeding automobiles. With overcrowded roads there is nothing surprising if accidents and road rage cases are on rapid increase."

"Now, to those travelling in big vans and costly cars, there is nothing like the right or wrong side, so long as they have their way," Shamsher added irritably.

"Shamsher, people of our age who have seen India changing from practically nothing to abundance now are proud of the country having unrecognizably changed. But don't you feel that development has gone lopsided in many ways. Haven't we failed in stopping aberrations from creeping into the system?" Jagan Babu pointed towards lacunae in implementing development projects.

"Very true. Material progress, howsoever marvellous, will lose its splendour, sooner or later, if there is no effort to build a value system with base strong enough to hold firmly the entire structure of material development," added Sharma agreeing fully with Jagan Babu on the issue.

Rakhi was fumbling to join issue with her dadus when she saw Shamsher Singh's son Narendra entering through the gate of the drawing room. She spoke as soon as the commotion caused by the entry of Narendra subsided, "I have been hearing your interesting talks, dadus, and wondered at undue concern for increasing number of accidents and road rage cases. When so many automobiles move on the roads, accident and road rage incidents are bound to occur."

Jagan Babu replied coolly, "Rakhi, we are not alarmed so much by the accidents, though their increasing number is also a matter of concern. But frequency of road rage is indicative of some kind of disease overtaking the country. That is something which cannot be taken lightly."

"Does it mean that we go back to the same old bullock cart age for fear of accidents and road rage incidents," said Rakhi stubbornly.

Ravindra, who was only listening so far, intervened to cut long matter short, "I think Rakhi's generation cannot get to the bottom of the problem. They have no idea how present day, with the best and the beautiful, has evolved through long, rough and bumpy path."

"Stop it, for God's sake! We have had enough of boring stuff." Shamsher was heard saying aloud to draw attention.

"Then, what do we do? Let us do something interesting," Pinky suggested.

To the relief of everyone, entry of Sandhya and Ratna carrying snacks with sweet smelling hot *pakoras* and a big thermos of hot tea with cups was the most welcome thing at that point of time. Pushpa Devi, Gayatri Singh, Prabhaji and Neenaji had already joined the company in the drawing room. While Sandhya was arranging plates and Ratna pouring tea in the cups, Rakhi was heard repeating, "Yes! Let us do something interesting that can keep us engaged. We won't let you play cards." Everyone understood what she meant by implication. While elderly ladies had settled there with their ears to the gossiping, Sandhya and Ratna withdrew to the kitchen to fetch more *pakoras* and *chutni* and to brief the maid about preparations for dinner.

"Ok. If all of you agree, I have a suggestion to make," said Shamsher Singh, "I am sure it will make an absorbing game if Jagan narrates his miserable tale of being lost at the farthest corner of the country and remained cut off from the rest of the world for around a fortnight. I remember Pushpa Bhabhi lost about ten kilos of weight during that period. Am I right Bhabhi?" He looked at Pushpa mischievously.

Goyal said philosophically, "Well, it was the case of a normal official tour turning highly adventurous by the stroke of luck."

To this Alekh added with a smile, "The moral of that trip is how a simple three days tour can turn a challenging adventure for Jagan and an agonizing experience for Pushpa Bhabhi, just by the twist of luck."

"Yes dadu! We will not interrupt," assured Rohan speaking for all. Jagan Babu began the narration in the mode of addressing an audience......

"Well, it was towards the end of Eighties, when I was posted in an attached office of Ministry of Information and Broadcasting, an important communication was received calling for inspection of the field office situated at the hill township named Anini at upper Dibang valley of Arunachal Pradesh in North-east India. During that period Anini was not properly connected by road. I was briefed about the assignment and was told that the inspection of the office with specific purpose was a day's job and that I could leave Anini next day to return to Delhi. Accordingly, instructions were issued to all concerned offices for coordination and travel and stay arrangements. Officer at Itanagar office was to accompany me. Accordingly, I was booked by air to Guwahati."

Jagan Babu had to stop as Rohan interrupted him. "Dadu, were you travelling that far for the first time?" he asked innocently.

"Rohan, I had travelled earlier to Bombay, Madras, Bangalore and such other big cities and even had been on long tours to the hills of Kumaon and Garhwal, but not to a difficult area like this which was not connected by roads at all.

"Ok dadu. Please continue" Rohan said submissively.

"Well, at Guwahati my colleague who received me left me at Itanagar. Next day I, with my colleague of Itanagar, started for Dibrugarh in the official jeep and, after having travelled on road for some distance, found ourselves at the bank of giant river Brahmaputra. There was no bridge on sight, and I had no clue how we would take further journey onward. While I stood at the bank and watched with fascination the flow of river water with all its sound and fury, my colleague bargained with the drivers of a huge, motorized boat to ferry us with our jeep. The whole process of mounting the vehicle on the open boat was a spectacular sight atleast for me. I then timidly followed my colleague and boarded the boat which shot up slowly as soon as we stepped on it. The boat moved midstream with threatening shakes and jerks with not a soul in sight for miles and when the boat tilted a little downward where jeep was parked, it was natural for me to have bumps in my stomach. We heaved a sigh of relief when the boat touched the bank of the river on Dibrugarh side and jeep was dismounted."

This time it was Pinky who could not contain her natural outburst, "My God, Dadu! When you were relating your voyage, I felt like travelling on the jetty with you with all the fears and accompanying thrill."

Pinki's remark caused tremor of noise for a moment. As the noise subsided, Jagan Babu resumed his narration....

"At Dibrugarh, we stayed at circuit house and next day, leaving behind the driver and helper with instructions to wait till we returned, we left for Anini on a helicopter, the Sortie service, which visited Anini once a day stopping over Roing on way, with passengers and urgently required material for inhabitants of Anini, the last town of Sino-Indian border. I travelled for the first time in a helicopter, and that too a sortie, with around two dozen people sitting and peeping with us downward through the narrow openings between the linings of the floor. We all watched with mouths wide open when the vast river Brahmaputra began to shrink visually into to mere flowing drains as the copter climbed up and looked around with subdued panic when helicopter moved between two hilltops. It was a forty minutes journey which was quite enjoyable by virtue of being adventurous from my maiden experience but not without lurking fear."

"Oh, what a fun. I wish I would have been there," cried Rohan with ecstasy. Jagan Babu ignored his outburst and continued....

"At Anini, we were received by local staff. We walked from helipad towards main township matching our steps with dozens of local passengers. The whole of the valley looked to me a barren dry landscape with population spread over sporadically. We were told that the entire circumference of the area could be covered on foot in less than an hour and that we could peep at the other side of the border from a specific point. Local tribal population was seen in their typical local attires and get ups. I learnt that Idu Mishmi tribe formed most of the population of Anini. Next day I spent the whole day in the office collecting latest reports and getting information about difficulties encountered by them in course of their functioning. On the third day, as scheduled, we prepared ourselves to leave and waited for the sortie to arrive by the middle of the day. But it did not come. We got the shock of the day when got the information that helicopters had been grounded and lined up at Dibrugarh to meet some emergency. For how long, nobody knew. This was the beginning of trauma for us. For the next fortnight, we looked towards sky expectantly every day but in vain. With every whirring sound we would rush out with our ears for an approaching sortie to only get back downcast and depressed. What added to our woe was total communication breakdown, as a result we were completely cut from the rest of the world. Administrator's office

which was connected to their controlling offices sent urgent messages, one after the other, almost every day about us, as senior Government officers held up, but they too seemed helpless in the matter. With every passing day we were getting accustomed to our pitiable condition and, in order to keep our nerves intact, we killed time by reading books and working on the report to be submitted on my return to Delhi office. There was nothing like a club or a hotel where one could spend wholesome time. Because sortie was not coming with supplies, we were living on scarce commodity like couple of potatoes and the flour managed by the caretaker by using his good offices, God knows from where, but good enough for our survival. After perhaps a week, we had the opportunity to look at a new face when an officer came to stay at the circuit house. His presence infused some life into us. We shared our pathetic conditions. When he told us that his father expired a day before in Dibrugarh, but he could not make it to be there, I realized that our predicament was nothing before the tragedy that befell on him. On enquiring how he could know about his father's death, what he disclosed filled us with hope to talk to and apprise Pushpa about me being safe and comfortable at the circuit house. The officer was the Telecommunication engineer who was on tour to supervise installation of a telephone exchange at Anini. I naturally jumped up to the opportunity and he had the grace to immediately take us to the exchange site which was yet to be fully operational. When, after some technical manoeuvring by them, I found myself connected to telephone at my home in Delhi, it was nothing short of a divine blessing for me. It was only on my return to Delhi that I found that what I thought to be a divine blessing was a sinister joke played on me by Almighty through His earthly tools of technology. My otherwise natural voice when passed through the instrument assumed such terrible quivering that it had turn into a panic call when heard by Pushpa. After talking to me on phone, she sank into the pit of anxiety and remained deep down in the pit till I returned in one piece. She had suffered a massive loss of weight."

Jagan Babu stopped and looked at his wife with a wink while she looked back at him with accusing eyes as if it was a deliberate act of mischief on his part to torture her.

"Dadu, you have created quite a suspense. How could a simple telephone call be disastrous?" asked Rakhi. "In fact, Dadi should have been relieved and relaxed." Gayatriji, Prabhaji, Neenaji and Sandhya looked at Jagan Babu curiously to unfold the mystery. Jagan Babu explained ....

"When I began to talk on phone, the engineer asked me to hold for a second and briefed me to the effect that the system was based on microwaves and hence only one side can speak at a time while the person at the other end only hears. If both talked in a conversational mode, then there would be choking of the voice, say there would be voice jam. I advised Pushpa accordingly and talked to her about myself hurriedly for fear of getting off the line. My advice was taken amiss by her and since my voice quivered because of microwave system of operation, Pushpa thought I was in terrific danger at a risky terrain. To add fuel to the fire, people of my office or even relations and friends, instead of trying to assure about my safety, either talked to her too realistically that gave terrifying impression or appeared to her to be quite indifferent to her plight. Ironically, at the other end, quite conversely, after having talked to her, I found tons of weight off my head. Utterly frustrated with illusory feeling of being under penal punishment and with no hope of sortie arriving in near future, we gathered information about alternative means to get out of Anini and finding that landrovers plied between Anini to Roing, we took a chance, packed our suitcases and reached the area where we found an overcrowded Landover ready to go. With difficulty we pushed ourselves into the open area densely occupied by local tribal passengers. The vehicle drove through the difficult roads on a high altitude, and I kept struggling hard to prevent myself from getting foisted on others. It was a highly terrifying and torturous journey but the hope that we would get normal bus from Roing helped me to sustain the tedium. Never before in my life I had felt as relieved as when we dismounted from the landrover. The entire journey was a tight rope walk for me. We made it to the residence of the local officer who had seen us off from Dibrugarh and whose address I found in the list of local contacts. Luckily, he was at home. He jumped with surprise to see us since he was aware about the suspended service of the sortie. The first thing that he did was to ensure that we boarded the sortie that very day on its return trip from Anini to Dibrugarh via Roing. We laughed at the irony. We were fated to bear the torturous and hazardous trip on landrover as a feat of forced adventure whereas sortie had run parallel to our road journey. Anyway, we travelled to Dibrugarh on sortie and had another shock when we learnt that there was total strike in Dibrugarh. Next day I was somehow dropped at the airport by my colleague who left for Itanagar after seeing me off for Guwahati. From

Guwahati I took the flight for Delhi through special efforts of my colleague there. On reaching home at Delhi I had to be at the receiving end, held responsible for the loss of Pushpa's weight by the gathering of well-wishers."

It was now Pushpaji's turn to speak. "Nobody can imagine my condition. He had said he was going on tour for three days and there was no clue for around fifteen days where he was and how he was. Enquiries made in his office evoked only weird and fearful description of the place which left me imagining only the worst. Others took it to be a normal trip with not a care about it. Naturally, it was hell for me. I did not know where to go and what to do."

"Frankly, those who could have been helpful were themselves in dark, whether they were office people or friends and relations. I agree that Bhabhiji needed words of assurance which perhaps she did not get. That would have helped her to keep up her nerves," Mahesh Goyal commented with a touch of sympathy.

"But Dadi, I wish I was there to see your face when dadu returned from the tour," said Rohan.

"I saw your dadu on his return, Rohan. His complexion had become unusually dark," said Alekh.

Sandhya and Ratna who had gone back to the kitchen, leaving others talking animatedly, called all of them after a while for dinner and they walked to the dining area gossiping merrily. It was almost midnight when they finished the dinner and got up to leave.

"Jagan, we will now meet on your return from Mumbai. Okay, have a comfortable journey and nice time there, all of you. Enjoy the marriage celebrations," Shamsher Singh said, and they were seen off as soon as the cab arrived. Goyal and Sharma stayed a little longer and left after some time with their families.

★ ★ ★

BACK HOME FROM MUMBAI

The train arrived at the New Delhi Railway Station, and they got down from the compartment, all the seven of the family members, following one after the other, gathered luggage on the space at the platform facing the door and watched enviously the whole lot of the passengers moving in a flock towards the bridge with their suitcases dragged on their tiny wheels. While others were seen moving, they were stuck up because two suitcases with them were too big and too heavy to be dragged without wheels. They naturally looked for the help and kept standing helplessly waiting for a porter to approach them. But none was in sight.

After a long wait, a porter passed their way and Rohan and Pinky jumped to practically hold him physically. He did stop but only to bargain an amount that sounded too exorbitant to be agreed to. While Ravindra's eldest daughter, Rakhi said nothing, Pinki and Rohan were inordinately vociferous in expressing their displeasure at the stubborn approach of their father who allowed the porter to slip away. For them, every minute of waiting on the platform was torturous. They were irritated at their father's refusal to engage a porter who they wanted to be engaged irrespective of what they asked for.

And all this while, dressed in an outfit that suited his frail and straight body, Jagan Babu stood erect like a pole under a nearby lamppost. Though seemed detached the way he stood at a distance from the rest of his family, he watched the scene with restless eyes betraying seething irritation at the changed scenario on the platform.

He recalled how flocks of porters swarmed on platforms after trains would stop at stations. He felt sad how the precious help which was once traditionally available seems to have withered away gradually. It was not that he was not aware about the reasons for erosion of this precious facility available at railway platforms. He knew too well that coming up of 3-tier reserved bogies and A/C compartments, with provisions of beddings on berths and pantries attached with most of the long-distance trains, have forced passengers to travel with easily cartable luggage. Naturally, in due course, suitcases fixed with tiny wheels replaced traditional huge steel trunks and holdalls which were being earlier carried by only professionals of sturdy necks and stout shoulders of porters called *coolies*.

At last, a porter agreed to an amount which sounded reasonable and they too could join the moving crowd which, by then, had thinned down considerably. They came out of the station, hired a taxi that charged the amount which was equivalent to a month's decent earning for millions a few decades ago.

All the while on their way, the old man remained silent, watching with restless eyes from the window of the taxi lazy movement of traffic. Irritated by the pace of his taxi which was running at the speed of a bicycle, his mind reflected on drastically changed pattern of traffic movement on the road within a span of a few decades.

Oh my God! While branded cars are now swarming on roads like hordes of sheep, every Tom Dick and Harry can be seen behind the wheels using them shamelessly even in crowded markets just to purchase half a dozen bananas or a few pieces of tomato, as if they are not cars but bicycles, obstructing flow of traffic unmindful to immense inconvenience caused to the people. A few decades ago, we had only Fiats and Ambassadors. Car-owners were on fingertips then. While he was enamoured of feats of achievements, he lamented the worsening traffic conditions which was getting out of control with around a lakh of automobiles added every year to over one crore registered vehicles plying on roads in Delhi. He laughed at the irony that while e-rickshaws were introduced to wane out gradually inhuman practice of manually pulled rickshaw, the lack of road sense on the part of e-rickshaw drivers is only adding to worsening traffic conditions on the roads. There used to be frequent traffic jams earlier, but they were mostly because of bottlenecks on narrow roads, but now, even feverish chase, by expanding surface infrastructure by broadening and building roads, constructing new bridges, flyovers, and underpasses, is not able to catch up with fast increase in numbers of automobiles on roads.

As the taxi reached their colony, Jagan Babu's trail of thought broke down. Once at home, their tiredness went off like scent in the air. Everyone was cool and relaxed. They all freshened themselves quickly to be at the dining table for breakfast.

Jagan Babu after having freshened, walked in his study room and, before he was called for breakfast, he stretched his legs on his armchair and, traffic being uppermost in his mind, he recalled some funny moments of his childhood that he spent toiling with a parked car with longing to have it someday.

He recalled how fascinated he was to see for the first time a car standing near the gate of his house and he, alongwith one of his cousins, kept examining its unique shape from all sides and angles. Since its door was not locked, they sat by turn on steering wheel enjoying the mock drive. The car belonged to one of his relations, senior engineer in irrigation department, who had come to call on his grandfather. That was the time when owning a car was a prestige symbol. Later, at the beginning of his career in the Government, when a jeep was attached with him, it was fulfilment of his longing that he had nurtured in his childhood. After coming to Delhi, at the end of Eighties he purchased a second-hand Fiat which was used only on weekends to visit relations and friends, as otherwise he had official transport facility. It is a different matter, he thought with a smile, that his car had to be pushed to enliven its battery. Prior to Fiat he had scooter, Vijay Super, which at times used to carry the whole family of five. After Fiat became too old, he purchased Maruti 800 which was changed with bigger model around 2009. He laughed at the thought that even in Seventies total number of passenger vehicles sold annually was less than one week's sales today. And now the roads and parking lots are flooded with cars of different models.

There was knock on his door to remind him that breakfast was ready. He got up and walked towards the dining table.

★ ★ ★

During the period Jagan babu was in his study room lost in his thoughts, Ravindra was at the receiving end from his son and daughters at the dining table. He was being grilled by them for making them wait torturously at the railway platform.

"Papa, why did you not engage the porter? We know money was not the reason. What was it, then?" Pinki asked him as if cross examining him in a court of law.

Ravindra thought for a moment and then replied in a hush hush voice, "Not money. I could have shelled it out considering our compulsion but for your grandfather who wouldn't have liked it."

"Why?" Rohan joined Pinky, looking cautiously towards the study room.

"You see, Babuji would not care for the money either," Ravindra said in an undertone to dispel any wrong impression about his father. "He was quite liberal with it in his heydays. But he is the last man to allow anyone to push him to the wall. In such a situation he reacts like an injured tiger. And that exactly was the situation there. The way porters bargained it was blatant exploitation of our helpless situation."

Rakhi as a mature person had a different take on the issue. She asked, "Why such a situation has arisen when porters have to ask for exorbitantly high amounts? Why their charges can't be regulated by the railway authorities?"

"Well, earlier, even during my childhood days, say not of your dadu's times, platforms were flocked by porters called *coolies* because people carried heavy luggage, which included big steel boxes and holdalls, in addition to bags in different sizes. Those were the days when we had our own bedding for the night travelling and trunks also had to be big because we normally went to stay with close relations for long durations. Naturally, not a single porter was left unengaged during those days. Now, the picture is different. Eighty percent of the travellers do not need the help, as they carry suitcases fixed with wheels and beddings are provided in most of the long-distance trains. Naturally, coolies now extract from whoever they can to make up for their losses caused to them by remaining non-engaged train after train. Or else they would starve with their families," he said with a touch of pathos in his voice.

"Papa, what was that you called 'holdall'. Dadu also made a passing reference to it in the compartment of the train while narrating about journey in his childhood. I heard this word for the first time," asked Pinky innocently.

"You see, holdalls were sold in the market as it was a household requirement in those days. It was made of thick waterproof tarpaulin with space so created therein through its sizeable cuts at both ends of its length that the entire bedding including quilt and pillows could be folded and pushed to be finally rolled and bound by leather belts. Look here, it is like this." Ravindra picked up a notebook from the side table and drew a sketch of both, the inner as well as the folded form of a holdall while describing shape of holdall. They stopped as they saw Jagan Babu coming from his study room.

"So finally, we are at home," said Jagan Babu as he settled down on his chair, picked up a plate and began to put butter on the toasts. He broke the silence which had engulfed the dining area at his footfalls.....

OVER CLATTERING WHEELS

In fact, Jagan Babu was ill at ease eversince he had boarded the train at Mumbai. The family had a compact space with seven berths reserved in proximity in AC-3 Tier compartment. Pinky and Rohan were having fun time to themselves on the upper berth facing the berth of Ravindra where he was lying lazily. Ratna shared space with her mother-in-law on the lower berth facing Jagan Babu's berth where he was sitting in a half lying position. Rakhi was lost in her own world sitting at the corner of the side berth fiddling with pages of a novel in her hand. At the other end of the same berth sat the occupant of the lower berth who first shuffled the pages of a newspaper and after finishing it, put it aside, took out a book and got busy reading it. Though in the precinct of that cabin, he was the only outsider, with impressive genial face and intelligent roving eyes, he did not seem to be an odd man out. He was almost of the same age as Ravindra.

It was not that Jagan Babu was travelling in an AC compartment for the first time. However, every time he travelled in modern day comforts of AC compartment, he felt strangely caged with not a breeze of fresh air available to him, something which was in abundance when he used to travel as a teenager in unreserved compartments. Cozy atmosphere inside AC compartment, while gave immense comfort and relief to others, Jagan Babu had tough time reconciling with what he felt was suffocating atmosphere closed as it was from all the four sides.

Lying on his berth, as the train had picked up speed after its departure at 11.15 a.m. from Bandra Terminus, he closed his eyes and got lost in the flow of what was now a dream with shades of pleasant and unpleasant colours. He was caught in a wistful nostalgic bout.

He found himself sitting by a window of the compartment with his brothers and sisters and watched the guard in his typical navy blue uniform whistling and waving green signal of cloth tied up with a stick and the train leaving platform with deafening sound of whistles mixed with dragging noise of steam from engine reverberating in the atmosphere. As the train left the station and picked up speed, they watched with fascination the moving landscape, farmers and their women folk tilling soil, heaps of harvested grain kept for hashing, cattle with their calves grazing here and there, and he competed with his brothers and sisters in counting trees and telephone poles which passed one by one as they watched them through the window. When the train stopped at midway stations, the commotion that overtook the platforms with the entry of the train, with babbles of voices from porters, vendors and, of course, passengers running helter-skelter to board the crowded compartments, resounded in his memory as he watched porters, with steel batches on their red shirts, flocking whole of the platforms on arrival of the train. He saw platforms turning into playground of multiple noisy activities, from vendors selling persistently in loud voices hot tea in earthen cups and eatables of varied varieties while moving from compartment to compartment, groups of passengers entering compartments with heavy luggage on heads of porters, some pushing baggage with children through main gates, while some others using open windows to push their luggage and family to occupy seats in already occupied space in the compartments.

He woke up from the reverie with a jerk as the train stopped with hissing noise of a slowing engine and he expected the same vibrant images of his childhood platforms floating in his mind with all the cacophony of voices of passengers and vendors. But alas, the translucent barrier at the window cruelly dashed his hope.

But, while he felt fascinated in recalling things which made his railway journeys in his childhood days full of thrill, he did not lose sight of things which made them tedious, uncomfortable and immensely difficult. He remembered every bit of hardship that he had to bear while travelling in trains those days.

Now he no longer has to run on the platform to bring pails of water, looking restlessly, with cautious eyes,z at foisting of green flag in the hand of the guard, and signal in the yard, while picking up eatables hurriedly from amongst the multiple hands of other customers. Now, sitting on one's seat in the compartment, one can have everything needed from potable water to snacks, lunch and dinner. Only, one has to plan the journey quite in advance to ensure confirmed reserved berths. A few decades ago, before the entry of computer on the scene, he had to spend hours standing in queues at the reservation windows for confirmed tickets, if he was lucky enough to get it. But if he could not get it into confirmed category, he had to go back with waitlisted ticket to be in queue once again for returning it. As against instant confirmation of seats/berths on-line now for return journey as well, it was an uncertain torturous wait those days. But it was the cacophony of voices on the platform that provided a kind of pleasant rhythm which he now misses despite apparent discomfort involved in travelling those days.

As Ravindra had seen him withdrawing from the window with a sigh, he came down from his berth and sat beside him followed by Rakhi, Rohan and Pinky who joined them picking up packs of chips as the vendors passed through the passage. Pushpa Devi was already sitting on the berth facing Jagan Babu with a magazine in her hand. As all the four elders sipped their tea, there began between votaries of three generations an array of interesting talks.

"Dadu, I know it is natural for you to remember your childhood days. But don't you feel that we live now in much better times than you lived those days when, as you yourself have said, even a small journey of around fifty miles used to be extremely tiring and awfully troublesome in many ways?" said Rakhi.

"Yes, you are right Rakhi. There is no denying that everything has changed in these seven decades dramatically," replied Jagan Babu without any hesitation. "And who does not like comforts and luxuries of the present against the odds and hardships of initial years after attainment of freedom when the country was struggling to usher in an era of ease which was quite off the mark then. But you know that there is always love for things which are associated with one's childhood. You will understand it when you reach my age."

"Dadu, I agree. But why is there this kind of intense pining for the days gone by when everything is fine now? Isn't it like torturing oneself for nothing?" insisted Rakhi.

Jagan Babu knew it was difficult to make them feel the way he felt on these matters. He said as convincingly as he could, "Well, you are right. But I am also not wrong. I will try to explain how I felt when I travelled in my childhood, and you can make out why it was fascinating to me."

"Yes, dadu. That is what we want to understand," said Rakhi seriously.

"I will talk about travelling by train those days and that should bring forth the difference. Our movements by trains were usually on short trips within the state of Uttar Pradesh, say, from Bareilly to Lucknow and back, as there lived our close relations, or from Bareilly to Moradabad and back where my father and two of my uncles were posted serving in various positions in railways. Once in a year it was our trip to Pilibhit which used to be unusually exciting because we all would wait all through the year for our schools to close for summer vacation, as we had our annual scheduled trip to my maternal home. You can imagine the thrill and excitement that we had as the days for visiting these places arrived," Jagan Babu began to narrate with a smile.

"And when the fateful day would arrive," he continued enthusiastically, "you cannot imagine the level of my excitement for travelling by train. The thought of meeting nears and dears, particularly cousins of my age, no doubt, was a great attraction, but what filled us with real thrill was the fact that we would sit by the open window of the running train, peeping down and out at the fast moving wheels, watching with excitement merging of tracks which would seem to be running with the train and then getting mysteriously out of sight. It was great fun watching some other train overtaking ours on a parallel track as if two trains were competing in a race. You cannot enjoy this kind of a fun sitting in closed compartment like this. You cannot count telephone poles as did we while sitting by the window. In fact, rhythmic movement of trains was fascinating enough to make us forget about any physical discomfort involved in undertaking journeys." Jagan Babu stopped to listen to Rakhi who wanted to say something.

"That is understandable, dadu. What I find surprising is outright rejection of all these wonderful things which make life much better and finding everything of your childhood enjoyable," Rakhi did not hesitate to express her observation bluntly.

"No, beta, no. I do not expect any one to refuse to see what can be seen even by a blind man. Nobody can deny that in preceding seven decades life in every field has changed for the better. I was only trying to say that since we had not heard of air conditioner and other similar present-day items of comforts, we didn't miss them. For us the natural air getting in the compartment, if the weather was good, was far more refreshing than the artificial air thrown by air conditioners. Yes, in summer it was indeed uncomfortable. You see, these things are relative. Even now there are millions who travel struggling the same way as I did in my childhood because of overcrowding despite all round development of railways in almost every area of travelling from ticketing to catering and bedding and so on."

"Dadu, much of what you have said has only confused us. Is it not a fact that there is more of affluence now than it was during your times? Why should you then bemoan remembering the days of your childhood, which were full of want and misery. We are really surprised," Rakhi seemed adamant to dig contradictions in her dadu's statement.

"I think, Rakhi, you will understand it better if you will let me complete the narration about my travelling experiences in my childhood. I will come to your point a little later," assured Jagan Babu.

"Okay, dadu!" said Rakhi.

Jagan Babu then took up the left out part of his narration, "You see, we as children counted days for the approaching date of journey and watched our parents selecting our dresses and clothing to be kept in a big tin box and small suitcases and collecting beddings to be packed in a holdall. While preparation would start days before the date of journey, process of finally packing boxes and binding of holdall would be done only a few hours before the time of departure of the train. And it used to be something to be seen when every one of the family was practically racing against time to complete the packing. The most interesting part used to be binding of the holdall with leather belts provided for the purpose after the whole lot of material had been placed inside and it was rolled to be finally bound which entailed physical struggle practically by all members of the family as bulk and bulge of the holdall normally evaded the limited scope of the leather belts in terms of its length. And then would start the process of withdrawal to adjust with the sizes of the belts. And similar was the case with the box which would refuse to be closed and hooked to be locked even when all of us would stand on it to put pressure unless the ruthless process of discarding garments was completed under wails and protests with every eye fixed on the wall clock, whose cruel hands were warning aloud that the time was running out."

"Interesting, very interesting", cried Rohan as Jagan Babu stopped to heave a sigh.

"And then, keeping the time margin after all of us were ready, our traditional Mohalla horse-driven-cart called *Tonga* was called in and, as soon as the galloping sound of the horse stopped at our big gate, we would rush with the luggage and hurriedly push it into the spaces below the seats and would climb and settle on front and rear seats. Now, we watched Chacha Shamshuddin with batted eyes, climbing with his heavy bulk, and the frail horse protesting against injustice done to him. But it was all over in a few seconds and the horse was running briskly on the metalled road. We would normally reach station sufficiently in advance because that normally helped us to occupy berths with luggage properly adjusted as the train started from there only," Jagan Babu was now ready to reply to Rakhi's query.

"How interesting! I am hearing gallops of the running horse," remarked Rohan enviously.

Jagan Babu ignored Rohan with a smile and asked Rakhi, "Rakhi, what was that you were asking me? Can you repeat your question?"

While Rakhi was reframing the question she had asked earlier, the gentleman sitting on the side berth got up and walked towards the toilet. There was silence for a while which lasted a little longer as the gentleman on return, instead of going back to his side berth, sought permission to join discussion which he was finding very interesting. Jagan Babu looked up at him with searching eyes for a moment and then with a smile welcomed him in the area where he was accommodated quickly.

"Thanks, sir," he addressed Jagan Babu, "I am sorry for inconvenience to all of you, but I could not resist the temptation to join such an enlightening talk. Please continue where you left it."

"It is okay. What is your good name, please?" asked Ravindra politely.

"Ashwin, Ashwin Mahajan," he gave his name and then addressed Jagan Babu, "Sir, when you were narrating your tales of railway journeys, my mind got engaged in recalling changing shapes of locomotives gradually from circular front to oval nosed Canadian Steam Engine and then to Diesel Engine and now to Electric Engine with plan to electrify the entire railway track. The transformation involved progressive change in energy position from coal to organic fuel and then to electricity. There have been expansions and strengthening of railway tracks and also replacements of old bogies by new ones providing for better amenities for the passengers. I thought to refer all this because of overall impressive progress by railways."

But Ravindra gave a different twist, "Well, this apart, I have to point at something which I always found fascinating since my childhood. Every train had an in-charge designated as 'Guard Sahib' who could be seen in his navy-blue uniform with red and green small flag of cloth in his hand and a whistle hanging by his shoulder. I used to peep from the window when the guard would whistle from outside his cabin, waving green cloth flag coupled with whistling, after the signal was down and then was thrilled to hear typical steaming sound of the dragging engine."

"Thanks, Ashwin, for adding important information. As for the Guard, he has been an institution by itself and continues even now, I understand, with variations necessitated by advancing technology that led to modernization of signalling system," said Jagan Babu, and then turned to Rakhi, "What was it, Rakhi, you were asking me?"

"Dadu, I think you agree that there is more of affluence now than it was during your times. Why should you then grumble for the old days which were full of want and misery. How could you be happy then as compared to now? We fail to understand it," repeated Rakhi.

"Well, let me first clarify that I am not grumbling at all. No one can deny that there is more of affluence now than during my childhood. From scratch in fifties to abundance now, everything in India has changed in these seven decades. Nevertheless, despite all round deficiencies and non-availability of material goods and consumable items, we found people then leading a simple tension free life," explained Jagan Babu.

"Very funny," cried Pinky, "with basic items of necessity almost totally missing, how could people live tension free. I don't understand it."

"It was because the tendency to economise was virtue out of necessity. People then did not grumble the paucity of things. They tried to manage with whatever was available. I heard my father saying repeatedly 'if you can' t have the best, make the best of what you have'. When I was in my teens, I used to watch many of my elders rubbing a used razor blade on a broken glass sheet to sharpen edge for shaving because 7oclock blade, the only brand available then, was quite costly. There was natural tendency to economize on everything to the extent possible. They used shaving soap cake as against luxurious shaving gels and creams, which, if at all available, were on an exorbitantly high price. They cleaned their teeth by using tooth powder or by using any other cheap and handy material like neem sticks instead of spending money on tooth brush and paste. For haircut, there were traditional barbers and concept of luxury saloons, furnished with all such modern gimmicks as would attract a well to do customer, was alien then. I said all this to bring home the point why people at that stage were contented and happy. If they did not have the shaving gel or electric shaver, they were not tense on that account. Housewives were happy to crush spices on a thick stone sheet called *silbatta* as against different makes of electrically operated Mixer grinder, popularly called mixy, in almost every kitchen now. There were no refrigerators and, therefore, eating material used to be preserved by adopting different methods like heating them repeatedly or keeping them in specially carved out mud utensils or hanging sensitive material on a net of rope called *chheenka* under the sky. They did not have then modular kitchen with cooking gas and gas burners and food was cooked on *mud- burners called choolah* and tin-carved burners called *angeethi* using fuel like coal, woods, wood dust and dung cakes. Later, gradually kerosene and electric stoves of different makes and cooking gas cylinders began to replace traditional *mud-chulas* and *angeethies* in the kitchen," explained Jagan Babu in detail to give his grandchildren an idea how different the life then was from what it is now.

Ravindra added cautiously, "I heard once one of my uncles commenting that youngsters now discard clothes like trouser, shirt and banyan on slightest tear whereas, during his childhood days, the housewives would stitch them to be used till it could be used with dignity. Perhaps, it was then a virtue out of necessity."

It was at this point that Ashwin intervened to say something. He looked towards Pinky and said in a soft voice, "Look sister, there is no contradiction in uncle's explanation. People in his time really must have lived far more happy life than our generations although they had meagre resources and limited scope to pick and choose. You see that the country had just then put off the colonial yoke and was facing acute teething problem during initial years after Independence. As against that there is now prosperity all around and my generation, which includes yours as well, have all the best living conditions after gradual development of the country in all fields during these seven decades and naturally we should be contented and happy. But we are not. While we have come to own everything that we need to live comfortably, even luxuriously, we are caught in a cut-throat competition, compounded by compulsions of Globalization. With laptops on our laps and smart phones in our hands, we have to be on our jobs practically for all the twenty-four hours. We do get huge salary. Do you think, caught in rat race with all that money, am I really happy? I have to snatch and steal time for myself and for my family. In fact, families, as a whole, have to bear the brunt in consequence and live in a state of constant war with circumstances created by rising expectations in every field from education to employment. So, uncle was correct when he made that remark," Ashwin was heard with pin drop silence.

"But sir, we cannot be prosperous without working hard. Service class apart, there is business class which is thriving while years back they too were struggling to settle down," Rakhi was not convinced by Ashwin's statement.

"Yes, you have a point, Rakhi. But there is a difference," Ravindra threw a courteous glance at Ashwin and then turned his eyes towards Rakhi before proceeding, "You see prosperity can buy luxuries but certainly not happiness. And present-day life is nothing but a mad race for chasing prosperity, a kind of perpetual struggle for survival. With no respite and relaxation, there is only the life full of tensions. I will not say there were no tensions then, but not the kind of tensions we have. I think now the perspective should be clear."

"Thanks Ashwin and Ravindra. You got me out of the trap. Not wholly, but partly," Jagan Babu laughed said with a loud laughter.

"Well, to be frank, there is no comparison between now and then. But I have no hesitation in saying that you are as poor as I was in my childhood."

Everyone looked at him with shock except Ravindra who knew that his father would pull out something magical from his basket.

"Dadu," cried Pinky. "Please do not mock at us with such confusing statements."

"No, I am not joking. You see what is seen by the naked eye is not always true. Apparently, you are rich and affluent and that is because of abundance of money in the country. But the fact is that there has been windfall of money during the preceding few decades which has proved to be more a bane than a gain. You will find my statement paradoxical, but the fact is that it has pushed quite a percentage of population deep into the pit of poverty."

"How? How, with so much abundance people will become poorer? Dadu, you are only throwing up riddles," said Rakhi.

"How? I will come to it later. The lousy money has created a very dangerous situation. You see, intoxicated by the lousy money in their hands, as obtained through hefty compensations in lieu of lands and properties acquired for development of infrastructure or through huge briberies, the irresponsible people and their family dudes have been defiling the neat social fibre by their irresponsible behaviour here, there and everywhere, from roads to residential areas and from homes to markets. The number of people who are sensitive to the pains of others is declining with every passing day," Jagan Babu stopped to only sip a little water and that was enough for Pinky to repeat the question.

"But dadu, how?" Pinky asked.

Jagan Babu smiled and said, "Relax Pinky. You see, the present day scenario is that carrots are being dangled before millions of people through attractive advertising in newspapers and on electronic media for novel products coming up in the market promising comfortable, even luxurious life for the people and, simultaneously, multinational banks have been liberally offering loans to their credit card holders on easy terms. Naturally, even economically weakest of the people are tempted to own things which they cannot afford even in their dreams."

"What is wrong with it? That is how living styles are now becoming better," reacted Rohan.

"That is where the problem lies. While they own things such as automobiles, television, refrigerators, music systems as procured through loans, they end up ultimately sinking deeper into the mire of poverty because paying back loan with interest eats away quite a chunk of their income forcing most of them to borrow for their day-to-day expenses. To make things still worse, there is a psychological factor. Barring a few sensible people, most of them are deluded into believing as if they wouldn't have to pay for dealings through credit cards. They are subsequently hounded by the banks for recovery of the loans with high rate of interest. They are thus caught in a vicious circle from which they find it difficult to come out. All the time they keep struggling to pay back loans which swell like swelling waters in a river ready to drown the borrower," Jagan Babu took pains to explain undercurrents of an invisible social problem in simple language what otherwise would seem to be incredible and exaggerated.

"But dadu, people have to have things without which life is dull and even painful," said Rakhi.

"I agree, Rakhi beta. We cannot stop the winds of change whatever the price we have to pay. To live a better life people have to work hard. Very true, but quite a lot of them, who fail to earn enough through honest means, slip into dens of crimes to chase the luxurious items of their choice by foul means," Jagan Babu insisted.

"Let us skip it, dadu. This is all a boring stuff. I am interested to know about your life. I mean how you and our granduncles and grandaunts lived in your childhood days?" Pinky changed the track of discussion. Everybody seemed inquisitive to hear about life as lived during initial years after Independence.

"Okay, I will briefly sum up and that should give you fairly good idea of our life," Jagan Babu whispered. "You see, it is a picture in total contrast with life now. There was no electricity then. Scooters, motorbikes and cars were rarely seen on the roads then and if we could afford bicycles of standard makes like Raleigh, BSA, Hercules or Hind, we were considered to be well to do, if not exactly rich. Horse driven carts called *Tangas* and *rickshaws* and, of course, buses, wherever they plied, were common modes of transport. Unlike today when travel abroad is quite common with sons and daughters of lakhs of Indians serving multinationals or studying in foreign lands, travelling abroad then was unthinkable and a mere dream. If someone travelled from, say, Uttar Pradesh to Bombay, he earned enviable title of 'Bombay Return'. Anyone found using desi ghee, bread, butter and eggs and wearing costly clothes like combinations of coat and pant in winter was looked upon with envy as a rich person. In case of illness, we would approach our family doctors at their crowded dispensaries and returned mostly with standard coloured carminative mixture with doses carved out by cutting small paper sheet and pasted on the bottle called *khurak,* accompanied by crushed medicines kept in folded papers called *pudias.* We depended on crowded government hospitals for treatment of serious diseases. Modern day huge private hospitals were rare and far in between beyond the reach of middle-class families. Well, I can go on and on," Jagan Babu hurriedly summed up a few facets of living pattern of his growing years.

"Enough of discussions! Now is the time for lunch," announced Ratna almost dictatorially. "Babuji, what will you like to have? I have some packed food stuff which we can supplement with some procured dishes of our choice."

"Same as for everybody here" replied Jagan Babu.

Meal served, all of them, including Ashwin, got busy in having their lunch of their choice which continued for about an hour with playful titbits between Rakhi, Rohan and Pinky as their side activity.

Lunch over, Jagan Babu lay down for a nap and all others retreated to their berths and engaged themselves in their fond activities from reading a book to hush hush gossiping.

Though Jagan Babu's eyes were eager to have a nap, his mind was so much shaken by discourse about the past that it was natural for him to be tagged with his nostalgic flash back. He was back to the days when he was a toddler.

Every word spoken by his elders then, as part of discussions in hush hush voice about the turmoil that existed before the country shook off shackles of slavery on the midnight of August 15, 1947 hit his ears with the vehemence of tidal waves of an ocean. Slogans like 'Muslim League Zindabad', resounded in his ears from processions on the roads between 1942 to 1947 demanding partition of the country and names of Gandhiji, Pt Jawaharlal Nehru, Sardar Vallabh Bhai Patel, Abul Kalam Azad, Rafi Ahmed Kidwai, Jagjivan Ram and many other leaders figured again and again during discussions amongst elders. But the name that he heard repeatedly because it dominated discussions was that of the architect of Pakistan, Mohammad Ali Jinnah whose pivotal role in creating a separate country for Muslims triggered the largest migration in human history resulting in the violence that ensued partition leaving behind harrowing tales of unbelievable brutality and barbarity, senseless killings, railway coaches coming stuffed with butchered human bodies and corpses piled at the railway tracks. As he grew in years he heard and read how, with a merciless stroke of luck, around fifteen million people, living normal family life with strong social bonding, were displaced from their roots, rendered homeless, their kith and kin lost and tossed in different directions, ladies subjected to unthinkable modes of violent sexual assaults, rapes, disfiguring, arson and looting. They lost their languages, ways of life, property and naturally their heirlooms. Their tragic tales of rudderless life became further poignant by heart rendering stories of their perpetual exploitation by those who fished in troubled waters, who believed in making hey when sun shines. Thieves and robbers were having the field day. He grew up hearing the new name 'Refugee' earned by the unfortunate lot who were uprooted from their homeland and some of them were seen by him settling in his neighbourhood as occupants of houses vacated by Muslims who migrated to Pakistan. Their tales of unbearable miseries had brought tears in his eyes. But later while moving ahead in years, he felt proud of them as he heard 'rags to riches' stories associated with them one after the other. He marvelled at their resilience and their fighting spirit and saluted their undying spirit.

Jagan Babu's thought sequence was broken by Ratna who stood with a flask full of tea and cups in hand. Sipping tea, he decided to skip the ghastly story of partition in his talks with his growing children who, in any case, will be in due course exposed to the events relating to the freedom struggle and partition that preceded the freedom of the country. They will then understand how tragic event of partition impacted the lives of their great grandparents.

Elders sipped the tea and the youngsters picked up cold drinks from vendors moving in corridor. They all resumed their seats and were ready for the next session. Nothing could be better in a long railway journey than to pass time the way they were doing.

"Dadu, you gave in brief some idea how you lived in your childhood days. That has only made us more curious to know in detail about the life as was lived then. We are in the train and have enough time, dadu," Pinky pressed her grandfather.

Rakhi, Rohan and Pinky were really enjoying the narration of the past by their grandfather as if they were hearing fairy tales.

"Dadu, please continue if you are not tired," said all the three in one voice.

"No. I am not tired. Okay, I will relate tales in bits about the life I lived since my childhood, and you will find them abundantly interesting provided you do not laugh at some of the oddities reminiscent of those days." His remark was responded with silence filled with curiosity.

"Well, how do you feel when you look to the old pictures of your papa mammy, nana nani, me and your dadi in photo album?" Jagan Babu was now in full form. "Do they not bring peculiar charm when you look at them in their contrasted images created by the spread of time? Now when I relate our living patterns in our past, it will be like rolling years in reverse reflecting glimpses of changed patterns at different stages of life."

"That is what we want," cried Rohan and Pinky in one voice. Jagan Babu paused for a while thinking where to begin from and then spoke.

"I, and so do you, belong to a family which was considered rich in the feudalistic sense. There were huge houses for us to live in and luckily ours was a joint family with dozens of brothers and dozens of sisters to play with on big courtyard inside and huge open field around. Each unit of the family lived in a certain portion of the huge housing complex formed of many clusters of houses which provided a natural opportunity to be together as and when occasions so demanded. We lived without any distinction of real and cousin. You will be surprised that most of the elders were addressed by us by a common name like *chachcha* was *chachcha* and *taiji* was *mataji* to all of us."

Ravindra and Ratna also began to enjoy the tales of the past with silent smiles, for they were in some way the part of the same establishment in their childhood.

"Oh! What a fun it must have been when you had so many of your age to play with and make mischief," Pinky reacted with obvious touch of envy imagining the whole scenario in her own way. Jagan Babu continued.

"Yes, I had a total of eighteen brothers and sisters living in the same premises, apart from some neighbouring lot that joined us as they lived with us like our fond cousins. And it was all fun and that is what I meant when talked of missing the old days. In the evening, after having played cricket and other local games when we used to return before sun set, we were so hungry that we would pounce at open almirah in the courtyard where were kept the loaves in a container along with other eating material. Without bothering to take plates from the kitchen, we would pick and rub two pieces of them with desi ghee and salt or sugar, turning them into rolls and gulp them with speed which we jocularly used to call 'tu chal mein aya' ('you go I come'). And our sisters had their own funny games to which at times we, the boys, would also join to tease them."

Rohan mischievously mimicked the gulping of mock pieces of loaf in his hands and his mouth making chewing sound rhythmically.

Taking advantage of brief pause, Rakhi came up with something different to say. "Where have gone these joint families now?"

"I think before I proceed further, I should reply to Rakhi's query because if I don't do it now we will miss something which is indicative of fast changing socio-economic pattern in India in the preceding decades," Jagan Babu was impressed by what Rakhi asked him.

"But don't forget to remind me to pick the thread of narration where I left it."

"Sure dadu. Where you said 'tu chal mein aya' and Rohan had his mouth watering," assured Pinky making every one laugh at her jocular style of assuring her dadu.

He paused for a while and then said, "You see, though as a result of massive transfer of population between India and newly created Pakistan lakhs of joint families were cast asunder, there still were large number of families in the country which remained untouched by the tsunami of partition," Jagan Babu gave in brief the background. "Now after the dust settled, the country launched Five Year Plans for systematic development and housing was accorded top priority after agriculture. In pursuance housing complexes were planned and executed by development authorities established for the purpose in every district. With easy provisions for housing loans, many of the erstwhile residents of unplanned and haphazard localities called *mohallas* began to gradually shift to the newly constructed houses built in colonies at the outskirts. Youths who left their homes in search of greener pastures later precured newly constructed flats where they took up job and settled. That is how gradually joint families began to disintegrate and turned nuclear . This does not mean that joint family system is completely wiped out. In interior areas of the country it still exists though things have been steadily changing there also," Jagan Babu looked around and found everyone attentive. However, Ravindra wanted to say something.

Ravindra intervened to add, "Though both the systems have their merits and demerits, the nuclear family system, besides being the call of the changing times, provides ideal conditions for living because each family lives life of its own without being caught in the whirlpool of joint family feuds and compulsions." Ravindra and Ratna had a taste of joint family when Rakhi was just a babe in arm. While there were innumerable occasions filled with mirth and laughter, they had to live through unpleasant situations as well quite often.

Ashwin, who seemed to agree with Ravindra, further added, "I have always felt that every family should live separately but not that far away from families of brothers and sisters and even close relations that they may find it time consuming and inconvenient to be together to laugh and weep together as the occasion may demand."

As the conductor passed through the passage, Ravindra enquired about the train only to be told that it was running late by a few hours.

After a little pause, Jagan Babu remarked seriously, "I fully agree with Ravindra. In fact, we have followed this system of living which is ideal. See we live in DDA flat procured by your Papa and your both the uncles live in similar colonies not far away. And look, we all gather quite frequently and have fun."

When Jagan Babu turned to pick up the thread, Pinky shouted, "Dadu, Tu Chal Mein Aya".

"Oh yes! I was telling you that in the evening, after having played cricket and other local games when I, along with my playing mates, my brothers and cousins, returned home before sun set, we were so hungry that we would pounce at open almirah in the courtyard where were kept the loaves in a container. Each one of us would struggle to pick and rub two pieces of them with desi ghee and salt or sugar drawn from the other shelf, turning them into rolls and gulping them so fast that it would look to many that they were competing with each other to outdo in speed.

"How funny!" exclaimed Pinky.

"It is interesting, not funny," Rohan corrected Pinky, "I wish I could be the part of this group."

"Yes, that is what I meant. what a fun! " Rohan clarified.

"But, dadu, I wonder why they were not being taken to task for devouring the whole lot kept for the family," asked Rakhi who was intrigued at their unreasonable behaviour.

"No Rakhi, it was not kept for the family which by then had already finished their lunch. It was normally the residue of the cooked-up material for lunch that was kept to be used when children felt hungry. Yes, once a while it happened that semi-cooked mutton or fish kept there to be cooked for the dinner was also devoured in the flow and that naturally evoked protests with wails and cries from those associated with cooking," clarified Jagan Babu with a mischievous smile.

"Papaji, this reminds me about the episode that you once related to us. I am talking about the Holi episode," Ratna who normally enjoyed hearing without talking drew Jagan Babu's attention to something which she had found very interesting.

"Oh, that Ratna. It makes me laugh even now when I think of it. But it will be spicy when I will relate it at the right occasion. Where was I? I was talking about our return home in the evening after playing games and devouring the loaves hurriedly," Jagan Babu stopped to recollect what he was talking and then continued the narration.

"Yes, we would then get busy with our allocated duties like sprinkling water to cool down the floor during summer by fetching buckets of water as drawn from handpump. The present-day water-works system of supplying water to consumers through pipes and taps was a farfetched dream then."

Jagan Babu stopped as Rakhi interrupted him to ask something. "Dadu, if that was the condition of water how did so many people of the family manage to handle daily chores of cleaning, bathing and washing of clothes besides safe storage of potable water for drinking. Water is something that is needed for everything since morning to evening. How did people in such pathetic conditions survive?" asked Rakhi.

"Yes, this was one factor that constrained the life of individuals in every family, particularly in large ones. It was not like today when with a mere twist of a tap water flows in abundance. At that time every drop of water had to be pumped out from the hand pumps or drawn from the nearby well to meet household requirements involving cleaning of the toilets to taking baths and cooking and so on. Now imagine how it used to be for everyone toiling to get ready for the day's work. There was natural tendency to avoid taking bath, especially during winter when arranging mere water was a great task, say not hot water, as concept of quick heating by switching on an electric geezer was nowhere in the range of imagination then. And that led to poor hygiene and consequent spread of diseases and, of course, high mortality rate." Jagan Babu minced no words while confessing the pathetic condition that prevailed then.

"And what about toilets, dadu? How then toilets were managed? asked Pinky abruptly.

"Oh my God! Don't remind me about toilets. As for villages, we all know that village folks have been going out in field for defecation. It is now that efforts have been made to motivate them to have toilets attached to their houses specially for the convenience of the ladies. In cities and towns there were toilets near the gates of every house and every morning a hired male or female sweeper would come to manually pick up the defecated waste material from the toilets from each house with the help of a broom and metal instrument called *Panja* and clean bathrooms with whatever quantity of water could be provided to them conveniently from hand pumps. Toilets were handled manually by the class of scavengers called in Hindi *Mehtar* and *Mehtrani*," Jagan Babu explained realistically how toilets were managed.

"O baba, besides being torturous, it must have been nauseating to go to toilet over and above used by others of the family earlier. Even the thought of it is repulsive," Rohan spoke with his fingers on his nose as if he has been pushed into one of the traditional latrines.

Jagan Babu added to make the story complete, "And if for any reason the sweeper did not turn up even for a day, the whole day we lived in unbearable nauseating condition. But necessity being the mother of invention, we invented different gimmicks like using ash to cover the dirt to escape the sight and foul smell."

"We cannot even think of living in these conditions," said Pinky, imagining what it meant to live with such repulsive compulsions.

"But one has to live when there is no alternative, no choice, Pinky beta," Jagan Babu said soberly.

"What about potable water, dadu? I mean hand pumps were the only source for drinking water as well. Was it not hazardous to health? Today we have water purifiers like aquaguard and ROs," asked Rakhi him.

"Source of water for domestic use, including potable water for drinking, was either wells or hand pumps. Normally people did not fall ill after consuming water drawn from wells because it was clean water as dug up at considerable depth. In addition, it was periodically treated with relevant chemicals. As for hand pumps, they were drilled quite deep to extract ground water which was perceived to be clean and safe. However, where handpumps were drilled at the high water level, chances of contamination were high because of mixing of rotten material seeping into ground water."

"I don't want to say, dadu, but we have no words to comment on such a wretched condition that prevailed then and you passed half of your life living under such conditions," said Rakhi with a touch of genuine sympathy.

"You don't have to be sorry now at this stage for such wretched conditions. You have only to understand the conditions under which people of my generation and their predecessors lived. Living was a constant struggle for survival for us and yet we lived contented with our lives and with a sense of commitment for a better future for our children," he said good humouredly.

"I know things had to be what they were," Rakhi displayed understanding like a mature person.

"You see those were early years after attainment of freedom from colonial rule for over two centuries and as the saying goes 'Rome was not built in a day', the country set in motion the process of change for creating conditions for wholesome living. But it was only with electricity and water-works system in place that things began to change rapidly and steps could be taken to build infrastructure which was basic requirement for decent living. And as gradually network of water pipes expanded to cover more and more houses, it became easier to replace traditional latrines with toilets having flush system," Jagan Babu indicated how process of change was set in to transform country from traditional to modern.

"Thanks, dadu for elaborating how process of change picked up motion. It is implied that advancement of technology played an important role towards improving living conditions of people including of those who were engaged in drudgery and dirty work," Rakhi remarked with genuine sincerity.

"Enough of it. Let us now go back to the narration where dadu left it. It was about helping the family in doing beds etc," said Pinki.

"Yes, yes! we would then help our mothers and aunts doing beds and other similar duties. But the task we usually tried to avoid was lighting the area before it was dark which we had to do by turns. I recall having performed the task number of times, reluctantly though. When it was my turn, I would fill bottles with kerosene oil from a huge tin through a pump and pour it deftly in lamps and lanterns and then undertake the process of cleaning glass covers of lamps and lanterns. The dusk waning and darkness spreading gradually, we would lit lamps and lanterns and take them to rooms, courtyards and to every corner of dark areas. While lanterns were hung at vantage points from where they could throw light covering maximum dark area, lamps of different sizes were placed appropriately, mostly on reading tables which were shared by two of us or even more. It was not like today when, at the push of a button, the whole area brightens with sharp light of our choice. Imagine the world before electricity was invented and introduced. For years, we lived combating the darkness. We had to study under dim light of lamps and used lanterns to go towards bathroom area."

"Oh, my God," cried Rohan. "How the feeble kerosene light could be shared by so many children to study?"

"But we enjoyed it thoroughly. We had to share the light and while whispering and fighting on the table, we were up with silent mischief. You see, despite all the handicaps, some of us could make a mark in our careers. Some amongst us excelled whereas some of us stagnated depending upon attitudes and capabilities."

"Oh, dadu. What a torture it must have been to be without bright light and cool air on hot days," exclaimed Pinky.

"Yes, it was virtue out of necessity, but we enjoyed it as a fun. All gimmicks to keep the house cool were adopted by us. We had no choice but to depend on hand fans."

"And what about schools? Without fans the students would be perspiring more than concentrating on their books," commented Rohan.

"In schools also we were not without fans. There used to be a very huge cloth fan in every class room hanging at the ceiling from one end to the other to cover sitting arrangements in a class and a man sitting back at the entrance of the classroom mechanically stretching by hand the rope tied to the hanging cloth fan which moved to and fro throwing air in all sides of the class room." Jagan Babu simultaneously explained its shape by the movement of his hand.

"My God, what a wonder!" said Rakhi soberly.

"But, if now I have to live under such conditions, it will be terrible, quite unbearable. Besides, those days, most of houses were built with huge open space and lot of greenery around with huge neem and fruit trees here and there. I remember to have spent with my brothers and friends most of hot days under these trees with cots to sit on and with hand fans to fan out the heat. While elderly ladies engaged themselves in household jobs like preparing for pickles and other eatables or knitting sweaters, we, the youngsters, would escape to adjoining fields to taste fruits after plucking them straight from the trees, besides playing games like *Labba Santh, Sapolia* and *Gilli Danda* incessantly around the lush greenery of trees and plants." Jagan Babu practically sketched a pen picture of his life as a boy.

"When did electricity come into your area, dadu? I know the country is too big and naturally it would have taken years. But how did you feel when, for the first time, you put your finger on the switch board to on the light and table fan to oscillate," Rakhi asked out of curiosity.

"Well, the process of electrification started towards the end of fifties and continued for how long to cover the entire country, I don't know. I witnessed the fixing of electric fittings in the whole of my house and, at the end, installation of electric meter by the electrician of the Martin & Co. As the entire house was electrified, we watched with gaping mouths the light emanating from the bulbs and subsequently we enjoyed basking in the air thrown on us by three wings of a fan rotating speedily on table. In the evening, the table fan used to be kept on a stool at the end of the cots placed in row so that everyone could share the air emanating from it. I had also watched with fascination installations of electric wires, plugs and switches in my school and, you cannot imagine the thrill my class fellows experienced when they watched, for the first time, air falling on them from ceiling fans hanging over their heads."

Having met the curiosity of Rakhi, Jagan Babu resumed the narration. "It was a sight to see and that is what I miss now, when after sunset big cots with beddings covered with white sheets and bulging white pillows were laid in rows in huge courtyard, shining under the bright rays of full moon while a big kerosene lamp kept at a corner and lantern hanging at the other side threw their own feeble lights. With darkness getting dense, elders would lie down on their beds inducing sleep through fanning themselves mechanically by hand-fans and we, the brothers and sisters, would have fun, between their rebuffs and rebukes, when we would not stop playing funny games or keep gossiping in hush hush tones sitting tight on our beds before being forced to go to sleep. Later when electricity was installed, table fans were used for fighting the heat. while big cots were placed in the courtyard, the open roof was used by grownups to have their beddings on the floor and lay there chatting and gossiping with eyes fixed at the moon that threw its white soothing light engulfing the entire area. Similar was the drill in the evening in summer at Moradabad where I was studying in class twelve with my cousins. There my father and his two brothers shared a rented house on first floor and when all the three families arranged their beds in a row on the roof on a long stretch, it was a fascinating sight particularly on full moon days."

"But dadu, that was all when you must be too young. How was it when you grew old enough to go to college?" asked Rohan.

Rakhi signalled him to wait while Jagan Babu went on describing in a flow important phases to beat the heat.

"Even after electricity was installed, the heat in summer would not stop torturing. No, it became more teasing because, electric fan threw hot air at an unbearably fast rate in summer. Now, necessity being the mother of invention, an important innovation to cool the heat emanating from fan was made by ingenious minds. It was the use of thick *Khas* fibre thatching to cover an area in order to create cooling effect inside a room at home or at office or in classroom of a school.

Wherever required, the areas were covered by khas, a pleasantly smelling dry grassy stuff which, with provision of sprinkled water on it to keep it wet, has the effect of cooling the area with accelerated air thrown inside by the fan. And later, since human ingenuity has no limit, the use of *'Khas'* was soon replaced by improved version of table fan with inbuilt system for cooling. It was known as 'Cooler' which has been in massive use so far and now are being replaced gradually by air conditioners after the supply position of electricity has improved drastically, but only by those who can afford to pay high electricity bills. This is the story of development where every step indicates a step forward to make things still better. And this is the pattern of development that applies to every field."

The train had crossed many stations but the family was so absorbed in the tales related by Jagan Babu that none bothered to know that it was time for the dinner. They ignored the repeated calls from Ratna until practically forced by her. They were on their berths after enjoying their dinner between pranks and jokes and were soon caught by sleep.

But while rhythmic sound of moving train began to lull Jagan Babu to sleep, an absurd incident during an overnight railway journey from Lucknow to Dehradun in Uttar Pradesh towards the early part of seventies began to nag him so outrageously that his eyes refused to surrender to lullaby.

He found himself standing in a long queue moving at a snail's pace at the Third- Class booking window of Charbagh railway station of Lucknow, while his eyes were anxiously fixed at the clock on the wall. Since train time was approaching fast there was pressure on him from behind and when he reached the window, there was feverish goading on his back to hurry up even before he had completed pushing three ten-rupee notes in the hands of the booking clerk, the cost of ticket for Dehradun being something around twenty five rupees. But he had the shock of his life when the booking clerk retorted saying that he gave him only two notes and not three ten-rupee notes. On his part he was sure that there was no counting mistake as he had only four ten rupee notes in his pocket and no more to create confusion in counting. However, due to rush at the window and pressure from behind, he had no choice but to shell out the last ten rupee note and obtain the ticket. He hurriedly came out with only a few coins which were insufficient to even meet the amount to be paid to rickshaw puller. It was the last day of his six-days official tour to Lucknow. But, as ill luck would have it, his pocket had been picked somewhere in the day leaving with him just four ten- rupee notes kept in his upper pocket. He had decided to catch the evening train and travel in third class giving up the temptation to travel in first class to avoid borrowing from a friend or a relative. He picked up a rickshaw and, since he did not have the change, he asked the rickshaw puller to accompany him to the booking window and he joined the queue to take the ticket. As he left the queue and approached the rickshaw puller after taking ticket, his pale face with restlessness to catch the train while engine was whistling betrayed to the innocent eyes of the rickshaw puller that there was something gravely wrong. Whatever coins he had he pushed into rickshaw pullers palm narrating in brief the tale of deception and his consequential plight, but the rickshaw puller, in a quick response, pushed back the amount saying he might need it on way. With one hurried look of gratefulness at the poor rickshaw puller, he rushed and entered a crowded compartment and settled at a corner on somebody's big box and passed the night with jerks and strokes of sleep, reflecting with drooping eyes, his brush with two contrasting characters who left lasting mark on him, one by displaying juggler's act of deceit on him and the other by displaying rare act of magnanimity.

He did not know when he sank into deep sleep. As the sun rays began to peep from behind the curtain of the window dispelling darkness of the night, Jagan Babu got up followed by Pushpa Devi, Ratna and Ravindra. Rakhi, Rohan and Pinki were asleep with not a care on earth. While Pushpaji, Ratna and Ravindra were busy in different morning chores depending upon as and when toilets were open to them, Jagan Babu was in no hurry to leave his berth. After a cup of tea, he sat by the closed window lost in the past with flashes both, painful and pleasant.

He could never forget the ominous hot afternoon of June 1954 when he, at his delicate age of fourteen, watched with weeping eyes heart rending scene of his father struggling hard for breath of life and finally giving up leaving the entire large family grieving with wails and cries. Later, on the day of an after- death-ritual, he recalled with a sense of pride, the loud rebuff from his uncle when he went to him to enquire innocently for his head to be shaved from the barber who was there for the purpose. He had shouted on him affectionately 'Go away, I am here, your father'. Though not highly educated, he was to him the epitome of highest learning, bestowed as he was with highly rational mind coupled with extraordinary bold persona. He remembered the day when his son, aged around 16, was admitted in the hospital in a very precarious condition. It was almost a gone case. And with no hope of his survival his well-wishers, out of concern for him, came to his uncle with suggestion to allow some renowned practitioners of occult sciences to try their hand. And short of being hit on their faces, they had to go back with their faces hung in shame. Uncle had declared at the top of his voice that he would let his son die but would not subject him to such an idiotic non-sense. That was the exemplary test of his rational approach to life and capacity to stand boldly to meet adverse circumstances with equanimity. His son had survived.

"Babuji, we are waiting for you for the breakfast," Ratna jolted Jagan Babu from his nostalgic flashback. His face clearly betrayed that he was lost in the memory of some painful but inspiring episodes.

Jagan Babu got up and walked towards the bathroom with his toothbrush, paste and towel. Rakhi, Pinki and Rohan also got up and got busy in freshening themselves. All this while Ratna, Pushpaji and Ravindra were left to themselves to use gossiping as filler.

"It must have been very tiring for Babuji to keep talking continuously for hours yesterday just to satisfy silly queries of his fond grandchildren," Ratna said with a touch of sympathy for her father-in -law.

Ravindra retorted with the vehemence that left everyone sitting there aghast and that included Ashwin who was shuffling the pages of newspaper.

"Don't talk rubbish, Ratna. Tell me a single question that they asked and that was irrelevant. As for Babuji, he does not get tired when he is in the company of his grandchildren. He enjoys narrating stories as he is good at telling tales," Ravindra seemed to overreact.

"Be ready, for today also. The train will reach New Delhi around 5pm. These girls have found a wonderful way to pass their time. And your papa is always ready to talk, whether it is a day or night," spoke Pushpaji with a smile.

"What about me, dadi? You left me out," cried Rohan while walking back from bathroom.

In a few minutes everyone got ready to munch breakfast and then began the new session when Jagan Babu was on his last bite. It started with the mischievous remark from Pinky.

"Dadu, tell us some interesting incident of your life which you consider memorable," said Pinky.

Rohan was not to be left behind. He spoke aloud excitedly, "Yes dadu. I am sure you have many stories which you may like to share with us."

"Yes, beta. There are lots of them. But we will talk about them some other time," assured Jagan Babu.

"No, dadu! Something, to begin with, dadu, while we are on our breakfast. Please dadu!" insisted Pinki stubbornly.

"Ok! You naughty fellows. But I do not know whether you will really enjoy it. To be frank, it is not merely the narration of an episode," began Jagan Babu, "It is the narration of a visit to a place which stuck into the recess of my mind as an unforgettable experience."

Everyone was now in full attention.

"After completion of my training, I had my posting at Dehradun in the year 1967 and within a few weeks, after my taking over the charge, I had to be on tour to Garhwal hilly areas for over forty-five days to work in coordination with a team of officials, equipped with all things required for performing our part of responsibilities. Our activities, besides others, included screening of 16 mm feature and short films every late evening in different parts of the rural and urban hilly areas as already scheduled for providing training to the people on civil defence. Accordingly, every day was a day of adventure for us when we worked till late evenings in the most difficult terrains. To reach interior rural areas we had to walk on zigzag hilly tracks for miles on foot with luggage and equipment carried by dozens of porters."

"Oh, dadu. What a fun it must have been to be moving like tourists," cried Rohan out of ecstasy.

"Quite true. It was a great fun to be at times on top of the hills and sometimes touching lowest surface of deep valleys," Jagan Babu marvelled at Rohan's capacity to visualize the scenario. "Each day was filled with fresh experiences as quite often we had to encounter most difficult situations like getting caught in landslides and roadblocks," continued Jagan Babu. "But since we were self-reliant with a vehicle equipped with everything to sustain us in the most difficult circumstances and had the company of others travelling in their separate vehicles, we seldom felt harassed by occasional hazards. Instead, we took hardships in our strides and converted them into tourist adventures."

"I wish we have such an opportunity now," Pinky said in a suppressed voice. Jagan Babu could not help smiling from the corner of his mouth.

"But the day that left an indelible impression on my mind was when my unit visited a hilly village, which though was situated at a broad valley surrounded by hills all around, but could only be approached after day long tedious drive on zigzag roads to take us through top of the hills to finally descend on our destination, a village in a valley. On arrival, we were received very warmly by village leaders who were waiting for us with local village folk. Their simple rustic hospitality I have not forgotten even to this day.

"As the sun was setting to spread darkness all around, our staff began to prepare for screening the films. The Elders of the village, however, requested us to begin the programme a little late, say, after people from neighbouring villages had arrived after their evening meals. While waiting in twilight on cots and chairs for people to gather we utilized the time in gathering peoples feedback on different issues of Government policies, an important part of our activities, and heard from them all about their lives, their vocations and their pastimes, everything that they had to say. "We did not know when the evening assumed the denseness of the growing night. We felt it only when in the pitch dark, there appeared on the horizon flickers of moving flames, descending gradually in congregation like a marching army from all around over the hills. For us it was a sight to see that got etched into my memory. We could not take our eyes off the marching battalion, the people from neighbouring villages pouring in from all around the hills with burning flames tagged in small sticks. And the process went on for around an hour.

"Then began the film show that lasted for more than three hours juxtaposed with talks as usual. And even after the screen went blank with sudden appearance of 'The End' to the film, people kept sitting as if frozen on their seats. A moment later, when darkness disappeared with light on from the bulb near the projector, flocks of people, sitting on ground, got up suddenly, as if defroze with the push of a remote, and began to move. Now, for us, it was the repeat of the same mesmerizing display of moving flames in thousands upward on the hills to which we could not take our eye off until the last row of images submerged in the horizon and disappeared."

"Oh, my God. What to say! We can jolly well imagine the entire atmosphere resounding with moving steps with burning flames in hands," commented Rakhi. Jagan Babu continued uninterrupted.

"As was the practice, after the film show was over, we talked to the people to know their reaction and what we heard then took us by surprise with an incredible revelation. There were a couple of elderly people in their late seventies who had never seen a film in their entire life."

And, recalling a parallel, Pushpaji quipped, "This reminds me about Sheela, the daughter of our landlord in Moradabad, who had come straight to our home after seeing Sohrab Modi's film ' Jhansi Ki Rani' released in 1953, and on being asked about the film, she replied with a touch of pathos reflected genuinely on her face, ' Oh didi, all fight and fight. They killed so many people just to make a film'. We could not help laughing at her ignorance after she left. It became a joke."

"Those were the different times. There were innumerable such stories of ignorance," commented Jagan Babu. "Illiteracy and poverty were the twin evils which had pervaded in India for centuries. Naturally, after attainment of freedom, it was the priority of the Government to remove illiteracy, as ignorance, being bye product of these twin evils, would wither away only with the rising level of literacy and the level of poverty reduced in the country."

"Dadu, kind of ignorance of Sheela relating to film was understandable at that time when cinema had not reached the households. Which are other areas where ignorance made people laughing stock?" asked Rohan as if ignorance was not something that should be taken seriously. He was looking for some ludicrous instances of ignorance to make him laugh though he avoided saying so clearly.

Jagan Babu did not miss the insinuation but said in a serious tone, "Rohan beta, do not take it lightly. Ignorance has been the biggest curse. It will continue to play havoc with the lives of the people until dispelled by the spread of education. Ignorance is like darkness of the night which is dispelled only by the sharp light of the day. I will relate just one instance in lighter vein to make you understand what it can do to a person." And he related while everybody heard him with curiosity.

"I was travelling once on a fast passenger train from Bareilly to Chandausi in Uttar Pradesh, which was around three to four hours journey during the day. Like many travelling youths those days, I would get down at every station when the train stopped and board it when it moved. With me was doing up and down a passenger who seemed to be from some village, and I thought he was doing it for the fun of it. But I was wrong. It gave me a severe shock when, at one such station, he boarded the train murmuring aloud in his rustic tone 'Oh, it is not stopping!' Alarmed by panic in his tone, I asked him once inside the compartment what the problem was and he very innocently said that he had unbearable pressure on his bladder but the train was not stopping to give him time to locate a place to urinate. Oh my God! The poor fellow was in pain for so long. I showed him the way to toilet inside the train and he looked at me as if I had shown him the way to heaven. And, in turn, when he returned from the washroom relieved, the look on his face was worth a million dollars. That was the level of ignorance in years immediately after Independence."

"It is only two and the train is running in time. I think let us grab a bite to sustain us till dinner. Ratna, have you sounded the maid?" asked Ravindra.

"Yes, I have talked to her. I will give a call to her while on way to home," replied Ratna. She took out eating material and served it.

While munching sandwich, Rohan asked Jagan Babu stubbornly, "Dadu, let us hear about your college life?"

"Okay, but before that I will tell you about my schooling. You see, because, unlike today, private schools with English medium were rare then, I was naturally admitted in class sixth of a municipal school after passing fourth class from an elementary school," Jagan Babu stopped to expect a natural query.

"And what happened to your fifth class, dadu?" Rohan was quick to pick the missing part.

Jagan Babu laughed aloud, and everyone looked at him with question marks on their faces.

Wiping his face with his hand-Ker-chief, Jagan Babu disclosed in conspiratorial tone, "I did not study in class fifth."

"How was it, dadu?" Rohan asked with dismay. Everyone looked at him with curious eyes.

"You see that year our country got Independence and, as part of national celebrations, we were given jump in our classes by a year. So, from fourth, I jumped to class sixth. Isn't it interesting?" Jagan Babu concluded with a smile.

"Very interesting," they all cried in one voice.

"For long I was butt of joke," said Jagan Babu. "The moment there was a slip on my part, pat would come the comment 'oh! he hasn't passed his fifth, naturally….'. And we would laugh at the joke."

"Any way, leave that apart," Jagan Babu Continued. "Interestingly, there used to be every year virtually a fair like atmosphere with thousands of students gathering at railway platform waiting for train from Allahabad which carried High School and Intermediate Board examinations results as published in the newspaper, and I recall the scenes of pouncing and snatching copies when trains arrived. Today one can have results transmitted through internet with every requisite information."

"And what else, dadu?" asked Pinki.

"In our times, our teachers carried a cane in their hand and we were actually beaten certainly by them for mischief and for class work quite often. Today, if a teacher touches a student of his or her class, all hell breaks loose on the teacher," Jagan Babu looked tired, but he kept talking to pass time.

"Dadu, I know one thing. A student in a classroom has his own dignity and a teacher is not supposed to hurt him in any way. Parents have a right to defend their sons and daughters," Rahki was adamant to argue for her generation.

"That is the problem, Rakhi. While your generation refuses for teachers the role of mentors of their students and that includes your parents, in our school days teachers were held higher than even parents as mentors of children. Well, say not of school, even when I was in college doing Postgraduation, I would shiver in my shoes on hearing commanding voice of any of our professors. I will relate only two instances. I think there is time enough to complete the story. Ratna, see that luggage is packed and nothing is left out," Jagan Babu was making sure that there is no last minute hassles when train reaches destination.

"It was the third day of the first year of my Bachelor of Arts English class and as soon as Professor Sharma settled down and opened the attendance register, we also sat down on our chairs. Emboldened by our success on previous two occasions, when three of us, sitting near the doors, had ducked out to have fun time at cafeteria, we repeated the same trick in prof. Sharma's class and slipped out after having spoken 'yes sir' against roll call. But that day we were not in luck. After the class was over, some class fellows close to us walked in the café and described dramatically how we were marked for punishment after being target of terrific wrath for over a quarter of an hour. Our mistake that day was that we forgot to calculate that once we ducked out, we would leave three chairs unoccupied whereas first thing that Prof Sharma did that day before taking attendance was to ensure that there was no sharing of seats. And, for the purpose he got chairs brought in specially from somewhere to fill in the shortage. Obviously, when he found three corner chairs unoccupied, he was furious. Prof. Sharma was a terror, not only for newcomers like me but even for seniors of post-graduation. Hence fearing the drubbing in next class, two of my co-offenders changed the subject, as there was margin of time for such a changeover. But I being in love with English language and literature refused to quit like them and prepared myself to face the wrath," Jagan Babu stopped to gauge the impact of his mischievous act.

"Very interesting, dadu. We never imagined that you could be a dare devil," Pinky said laughingly.

"That is not the end of the story. When you hear what happened at the end, you will recommend my name for some national award," said Jagan Babu jocularly and resumed narration.

"I sat in Prof Sharma's class like a lamb waiting to be butchered. But I had prepared couple of my back bencher friends to endorse what I would say when I stood up to defend myself. Prof. Sharma came and, while taking attendance, he stopped at the names of two defaulters who were naturally not in the class. He simply said in their case something like, 'oh, so they are not here'. And then came my turn. He called "Jagdamba Prasad" and I said, "yes sir". Fast came his lenses on table with a thud, symbolic display of his anger. "You had run away from my class last time?" "No, sir" I said firmly, "I was on leave that day.' "But you are marked P". "Somebody must have spoken proxy, sir. You can ask the class." And I virtually pulled by their shoulders two of my class fellows to endorse my statement. And his anger melted like burnt out wax. Mind it, fifty percent of class had girls and the entire class knew I was telling a lie. Nevertheless, I came out in flying colours like a hero."

"My God, dadu! You must really have been a hero," commented Rohan.

"No. I could be taken as a vagabond, a loafer, not a hero in any case. Don't take me seriously. I was a very shy and timid student," said Jagan Babu with a mischievous smile on his face. "Will you not ask what the second instance was that I wanted to relate?"

"Yes dadu," said Pinki.

"That is anti-climax. I heard after a few years while in my office in Delhi that Professor Sharma, whose mere appearance anywhere within college premises, would send students of even Postgraduates looking for cover, was recently beaten by students mercilessly so much so that he suffered for long with multiple fractures. I had tears in my eyes when I heard it. Besides the fact that he was such a lovely father figure and a very learned person, I had tears for such a low stooping down of a category of students who are supposed to be the leaders of the country in future. That was indicative of changing times for the earlier value system that had made us not only educated and learned, provided we had the potential, but also a good and principled human being."

Jagan Babu concluded with a sigh and others sat dumbfounded on revelation of an unfortunate episode.

'Frankly, it is a very complex problem that needs to be analysed seriously to find where things have gone wrong," Ravindra intervened to cut the matter short.

"You are right, Ravindra. To sum it up in couple of words, I will say only two things. One, that though we began our studies as children with *Slate* and *Chalk*, *Takhti* and *Budakka*, the white mud ink used for writing on wooden sheet called *Takhti*, given *G-nibs* to write on four lined notebooks for improving handwriting, we could, nevertheless, reach this stage of learning and are not way behind those who have the modern gadgets at their disposal like iPad in their hands and computer on their laps," Jagan Babu closed the chapter as the sun was setting signalling that the destination was not far off.

He sat by the window waiting for train to reach the destination. There was silence in the compartment now. But Jagan Babu could not help remembering the so called Kamchi of his grandfather and the cane of his teachers.

He recalled with awe his grandfather's kamchi, a thin neem stick, long and elastic, neatly chiselled, hung on a pair of pegs at the corner of the entrance to the gate of the main house. And that Kamchi symbolized his grandfather's authority over his dozens of grandchildren. Though he saw it being used only once a while, but its mere fact of hanging by the wall was enough to keep them all in awe of it. As he grew in years, he began to believe that a cane in the hand of a teacher is a symbol of filial authority. However, of late, some of the stories in the media about the suicide by school children following punishment by the teachers and the reactions of parents and society as a whole demanding forcefully abolition of corporal punishment in schools appeared to take away relevance of the old dictum 'spare the rod and spoil the child'. The Ministry of Women and Child Welfare showed its concern by legislating on the issue. He felt shocked at the developments as he very strongly felt that children should not be allowed to grow with their feet of clay. They should be physically sturdy and emotionally strong enough to withstand such situations as classroom humiliations. And it is the responsibility of the parents to infuse the sense and strength in their children with faith in teachers as their mentors. He laughed at the thought that words and cane can be reason for suicides because if it was so people of his age would have committed it at a mass scale long ago. There is no denying, he thought, that there have been a few amongst teachers with streak of villainy in them. But such teachers can be dealt with under existing penal laws. But to think of framing laws to stop corporal punishment and including in the ambit even the parents and kin is to take things a little too far. And yet something needs to be done to stop the menace, he murmured thoughtfully. If a stare cannot throw a scare in a child, nothing else can and that is the fact about which teachers and parents alike should not only be aware of but should endeavour to practise. Cane should nevertheless be in the hand of a teacher as a symbol of authority. Fear without respect is crushing and respect without fear is of no consequence.

He was interrupted by Rohan who saw him lost in thought. "Dadu, what are you thinking?" He asked him just to cheer him up.

Jagan Babu side tracked to avoid getting into prolonged discussion and replied with a smile, "Well I could never forget continued trauma that I had to suffer for couple of hours at the hands of my father once when I was caught doing a grave mischief as a growing child."

"What was it, dadu? Oh! What a fun it should be to hear about it," Rohan exclaimed with ecstasy and Jagan Babu obliged him to keep him in good humour.

"Sitting on an easy chair with pipe of a *hukkah* between his lips, a thin long cane in his one hand and the other holding his two tiny hands, while my father kept talking to his colleague sitting on a chair next to him, he would lift the cane ferociously as if ready to hit me, though the cane did not touch my body even once. Every time my father lifted the cane with a grunt in his voice, I shivered in my knicker. And this went on for over an hour which sapped my energy because of constant sobbing, tears trickling incessantly and, above all, the lurking fear of being hit any time in course of this on-going drama. And here I was today, a law abiding citizen, who could brave all the odds of time in his journey for decades, from exuberant youth to the age of a grandfather."

"But dadu what was the mischief that you had done for which you were being punished?" Rohan asked Jagan Babu.

"Oh, that I will tell you some other time as the train is now about to reach Delhi," said Jagan Babu. Rohan had to concede as there was no time to carry on conversation.

As the train touched New Delhi Railway Station platform, children quickly got ready. Ravindra and Ratna had already packed and pooled at one spot the spread up luggage hurriedly and when the train stopped, they got down dragging items one by one.

★ ★ ★

"So finally, we are at home," said Jagan Babu while putting butter on the toasts.

He had arrived from his study room to the dining table and while settling on his chair broke the silence which had engulfed the dining area at his footfalls.

During the period Jagan babu was in his study room lost in his thoughts, Ravindra was at the receiving end from his son and daughters while they munched light refreshment. He was being grilled by them for making them wait torturously at the railway platform.

Jagan Babu spoke as he filled his plate with snacks of his choice, "There is nothing better than being at home after all this hurly-burly of marriage celebrations."

"Yes, very true, dadu! Except the bitter experience at the platform, it has been a pleasant journey. But marriage apart, what really made our trip enjoyable was our return journey by train. We are still not out of the spell of magical sketch that you drew through your narration about your childhood days," said Rakhi.

No more questions were asked and nothing further was spoken. They retreated to their rooms to relax after a long journey.

Jagan Babu took his afternoon tea in his study room. He had taken down from the top of his almirah heaps of old papers to sort them out and was in the midst of studying a bunch of sheets when Rakhi came running from drawing room to hand over his buzzing mobile which he had forgotten to pick after his lunch. Rohan and Pinki made it too to study room close on the heels of Rakhi. They were silent till Jagan babu finished talking, but as soon as he put aside the mobile, his grandchildren shot questions as to what he was doing. "What are these papers in two heaps, dadu?" asked Pinki.

Jagan Babu explained to them what he was busy with and pulled out two sheets from the heaps of papers, one folded and the other a small card, and lifted them up enquiring in a mysterious tone, "Can you tell me what is in my hand?" Reacting spontaneously Pinki tried to virtually snatch them from his hand, but Jagan Babu held them back with the remark, "No, Pinky no! These are very precious papers and very old, hence slightly soiled. A slight rough handling and these are gone."

"What are these two papers, dadu?" asked Rohan impatiently.

"These are the letters written by my grandfather to his son, my father. These have archival value for me," explained Jagan Babu. "Before I tell you further about them, you can examine them. But handle them with utmost care."

Jagan Babu handed the papers one by one to them. He gave at first a 4x6 inches card with jottings on it. They looked at it from all angles but since jotting on it was in Urdu they could not make out what it was. He then gave them folded paper in bluish colour to be examined by them. When it was unfolded by Rakhi, they looked at the sheet now spread before them and found it full of written material in free hand. But since the written material on it was also in Urdu, they were unable to make out what it was. They looked at Jagan Babu with question marks on their faces.

Jagan Babu explained, "As I told you, these were the letters written by my grandfather to his son, my father. I have couple of letters written by them to each other in English also. I will find out where I kept them. My father and my grandfather knew English and Urdu. My father tried to learn Hindi at a later stage when I was in school."

"That is alright, dadu. But what they exactly are?" Pinki was unable to keep patience.

"Well, today when you have to communicate with your relations or friends, how do you do that? You write a message or a detailed letter and send it through E-mail or WhatsApp and instantly it reaches to the receiver on his laptop or Smart Phone. And the receiver of the email or message can respond instantly through the same mode. But during my school days, say until computer with internet and mobile entered in the country and expanded, people living in different parts of India were corresponding with each other through letters posted in the letter boxes. You know that at that time there was a vast network of post offices all over the country," Jagan Babu stopped to make sure that he was being heard with interest.

Before he could proceed further Rohan reacted, "Dadu, post offices are still there. What is strange about them?"

"Yes, there are post offices and post boxes as well. But while post boxes now stand empty as symbol of the past, post offices have been reorganized with various defined activities considering their established reach all over the country."

"How these two old documents you showed to us, dadu, were related to post offices?" Pinki enquired with natural curiosity.

"Okay. The 4 x 6 inches card with jottings on it, which I showed to you, was used to be called Postcard. Its one side full space plus half of the space on the other side was for writing the communication by sender and remaining half with stamp and lines stretched on it was for the address of the receiver. After writing address, it was to be dropped by the sender in the post box available outside post offices or at other places wherever they stood installed for the convenience of the people," explained Jagan Babu and stopped to take a sip of water.

"And these letters used to reach destinations. How dadu?" Rohan asked Jagan Babu.

"Yes. I will come to that," said Jagan Babu. "The blue coloured folded paper that I showed to you was called Inland letter. It had one side full sheet and half on other side for writing the communication and the remaining space with lines drawn and stamp fixed was for the address of the receiving end. After writing address it was to be folded and closed with gum provided on its specific side and then dropped in the post box. The post cards, inland letters and envelopes could be purchased from post offices by paying the amount equivalent to the worth of the stamps affixed on them. Envelops were used for sending letters or documents kept inside and then closed with gum on it. They were also to be dropped in the post offices after writing address on the cover. With post office stamp on them, they were the cheapest mode of communication earlier. The main thing is stamp. If weight of the envelop is more, then addition stamp is a required to be affixed."

"Dadu, that was the senders' side. How did it work at the receiving end?" Rakhi, who was hearing the whole thing with an academic interest, wanted the picture to be complete.

"You see the letters of all the three categories normally reached the destinations in most of the places in India in two to three days' time as the postal services involved transporting material to different places in the country through railway trains, further onward transportation by roads and to some distant places by air. The postal material, called dak used to reach first at the head post office of a district and from there postal material was distributed to different post offices of the district. Finally, the material used to be handed over to postman of each beat for delivering letters at the mentioned addresses," Jagan Babu tried to make his description as easy as he could do for them to understand.

"My God! It was indeed a huge task handled by post offices," Rakhi commented with a sense of appreciation.

"Yes indeed! Have you any idea, Rakhi, how money used to be sent from one place to the other? Supposing you needed to send money to your brother residing at Lucknow. You had to walk to a post office, fill a money order form and hand it over alongwith money to the official there who would give you a receipt. In a few days the money would be delivered to the recipient at Lucknow. It is different now. You can send money on-line in seconds."

"Really, how difficult were those days," said Pinky sympathetically.

"But most interesting was the post office facility for sending urgent message on telegram which was operated through telegraphic signal system. If the message was, say, 'your father seriously ill', the sender will write the message on a telegram form or even on blank paper with advice to send the telegram and pass it on to the post office and the sending post office would encode the message by using his finger on a machine creating tttt sound which in fact was transmission of message through coded signals to be deciphered at the receiving post office which, on its receipt would decode and reproduce the message on telegram form to be delivered urgently at receiver's address by a postman. This was then the height of technological advancement which was kept reserved for Government use for rapid communication purposes. Now, it is said that a piece of information can reach the farthest corners of the globe even before you tie up your shoelaces," Jagan Babu spoke to elaborate how critical aspects of communication were handled with scarce technological support through post offices then.

"How different is this country now from the one where you spent your life as a child and youth, dadu," said Rakhi philosophically.

"Yes, you are right, Rakhi. You see as a teenager once in fifties I was asked to use telephone at the residence of our neighbour, a government officer, the only one in the entire big locality and it turned out to be a terrible experience for me. As I lifted the receiver from the instrument, which was kept at a corner table like a black cat sitting thereon, and put it on my ear, the bark of the man from the exchange to ask the number to be connected hit my eardrum so hard that the receiver fell from my hand," Jagan Babu laughed aloud.

"But now we have our landline telephones with dialling system," said Pinki.

"Yes, in due course, with dialling system introduced, Telephone Exchange became automatic. And the process did not stop at that.

Today, a tiny toy called mobile with a miracle chip into it can be seen in the hands of all types of people, from scrap dealers and shop keepers to top officers and executives. This tiny toy, which is the miracle of the last century, is packed with varied mind-boggling functions broadly including email, multimedia messaging, camera, video player, word processing, internet browsing. It has a complete wireless access to almost every corner of the world," Jagan Babu concluded.

"Yes, dadu. With this we can now communicate at the farthest corner of the world, hold videoconferences, make financial transactions, seek information on any subject under the sun, locate places. It has alarm clock, calendar, and calculator," Rohan elaborated and displayed his knowledge with an air of pride.

"You have all distracted my attention from what I decided to finish today. Okay, I will put back the old papers again. I will sort them out some other day. Let us go to drawing room now," Jagan Babu declared.

★ ★ ★

BAND BAJA BARAAT

One day late in the evening when Jagan Babu was returning from the main market, his car had to stop only to join a long queue of stranded vehicles just before the turning at his colony's gate because a marriage procession had blocked almost the entire road. Huge Park facing the gate of the colony was the venue of marriage. He watched from his car *baratees* of all age groups dancing to the familiar tune of *band baja with* beats of *dhols*. The madness of dance lingered on until it was forced to stop and *baratees* began to enter the venue.

As the road became clear slowly, he could drive to reach his flat and tired of the *dhol* still hammering his ears, he settled to relax on his long chair in the drawing room. There was still time for the dinner. The fading cacophony of tunes of band baja baraat now stirred his mind with irresistible laughter to an incident connected with a marriage reception that he had attended in Delhi with his wife years back.

It was pleasant evening of February when he with Pushpa left for Rajouri Garden in his car to attend the marriage of the son of his old class fellow on being invited very warmly by him on telephone. It was after decades that he heard Harish's voice after he joined Airforce and held the position of squadron leader. Like him, he too belonged to middle class family and had struggled hard to build his career. It was natural for him to respond to the warmth of Harish and was keen to see him in his official grand position. As they reached the venue of wedding with best of understanding of directions, without navigating facility of today to lead them to exact location, he found a grand party going on with quite a good number of sophisticated guests. He entered the venue with Pushpa and, since they had covered quite a tiring distance on crowded roads, Pushpa lost no time and settled on a table with some palatable snacks as picked up from roaming waiters. She had never met Harish and his family and naturally was at ease whereas his eyes were wandering to locate any known face. Suddenly a serving man came near him and offered him whisky which he was holding in a tray with soda. He was tempted to pick one glass of whisky, but somehow stopped short of lifting it. He had not seen a single known face. Very discreetly he enquired about Harish as the host but he was in for a shock when he was told that the host was some renowned Punjabi businessman. He found the ground slipping under his feet as he feared that they could be caught as unauthorised intruders. There was not a soul to vouch for them. He whispered in the ears of Pushpa to discreetly retreat and together they walked out unnoticed to the parking spot. Out of the venue, he heaved a sigh of relief and drove to locate actual destination under torrents of castigating bits from Pushpa. Blood drained in these fifteen trying minutes returned to his cheeks. And now, the scene that awaited them was the anticlimax. They landed at a lacklustre spot only to supervise winding up process. Though Harish received them warmly and escorted them to be seated, they found themselves sitting in a row amongst thin boring crowd of guests comprising mainly aging lot and watched from a distance youngsters surrounding newly married couple before final ceremony of Vida.

The call for dinner jerked Jagan Babu from reverie and he walked indolently towards dining table to join others who had already gathered there.

★ ★ ★

On a Sunday when everyone of the family had settled on their dining chairs for lunch and Ratna, as usual, guiding the cook in the kitchen, Rakhi broke the silence.

"Dadu, I hope you enjoyed the marriage at Mumbai," Rakhi said for the sake of saying something.

"Well, it was very nice. Like marriages in Delhi, there also it was one day affair," Jagan Babu gave a crisp reply.

Before conversation could go further, Ravindra broached the issue of marriage of his friend's daughter on coming Tuesday. Sipping the soup leisurely, he stressed that Ramesh expects Babuji to join the wedding to bless the couple. He told him he would be coming tomorrow to personally invite him.

Jagan Babu kept sipping soup with his spoon and did not react immediately. A crease on his forehead betrayed that he was brooding over something which was not necessarily the issue of attending the marriage of Ramesh's daughter, Sunita whom he treated as his own granddaughter. After an eerie of silence, Jagan Babu responded with a smile, "Ravindra, if you spare me, I will be happy to be at home. I will make it at any other time to meet the couple. I want to avoid going because somehow, I do not feel comfortable in marriage parties these days."

While Ravindra assumed silence as he knew that Babuji being emotionally attached to Ramesh's family will not miss to attend the wedding, Pinki reacted and put the question bluntly, "Dadu, what makes you uncomfortable in marriages these days?"

"Nothing wrong in marriages. You can say I have grown too old to enjoy marriage ceremonies the way I enjoyed when I was of your age," Jagan Babu wanted to avoid stretching the subject by sheer comparison. He was aware that while basics remain the same, what has changed is the mode and method of organizing and celebrating different steps of a marriage.

Rohan, however, commented aloud, "I have seen dadu turning back with irritation every time he watched a marriage procession on the road."

They all looked askance at Jagan Babu, but he said without hesitation, "True, I do not like ladies dancing with men in the marriage processions on roads. But this is not the reason for me to be hesitant to attend marriages now a days. If dancing on the roads has come into fashion, let it be so."

"Then what is it?" asked Pinky impatiently.

Pressed hard he said, "I don't know. It is all so confusing now. The desire to show off family status eclipses practically pious undercurrent of emotions, and glamour and loudness overtakes the entire show. I had a baffling experience when I attended a marriage in Delhi recently. After unstoppable dance on the road, somehow the procession moved and as the barat reached the venue of reception, there came in sight series of reception spots, contiguous to each other, in a composite building, ready to receive half a dozen marriage processions, all at a time. The madness of dances mixed with unmusical loud cacophony coming from all corners made my stay there quite torturous."

"Dadu, we all know about space crunch in Delhi for marriages," Rakhi gave logical reason for going in for multiplex wedding complexes.

"I quite agree, Rakhi," said Jagan Babu. "You see, in my boyhood days, precious spaces to be let out as marriage halls, baratghars of today or lavish farmhouses were rarely available to even well to do middle class families. Most of the marriages had to be performed at the residential premises of mohallas which stretched to available open areas outside extending to even roads and lanes. You see, unlike today's marriages which are over in less than twelve hours, marriages then took three to four days from the time of arrival of barat till the departure of the bride. You can't imagine what a fun it used to be for all of us."

"But dadu …," Rohan began to say something but Jagan Babu interrupted with a smile, "Bachchon, you are dragging me in prolonged discussion. I need to relax after lunch."

"Ok, dadu," they cried in one voice and saw Jagan Babu walking towards his bedroom.

But as he stretched his legs on the long chair in his bedroom to relax, the discussions on the dining table trailed him like his shadow and he rejoiced and reflected recalling days of his boyhood when he attended marriages and enjoyed every ceremony with gusto.

Unlike today, when everybody is in a hurry and find leisurely time with efforts, people those days had lot of time to spend on occasions as important as weddings. Show off element was there then also, but in a limited sense. In those days it was customary to involve whole lot of community turning the ceremony into an occasion of fun and frolic perforce. Recalling the participation of relations, friends, neighbours on the occasion of marriages of girls of the locality, he felt proud at strong sense of community bonding, something which has now becoming a thing of past. In marriages now a days, especially in metropolitans and big towns, guests of the bride's side do not wait for the marriage procession to arrive. They start gulping meals and leave, one after the other, pushing envelop in the pocket of bride's parents leaving behind a very thin gathering of close relations and friends. In his boyhood days when marriages were settled in two different townships, nearby or distant, the marriage party had to travel to bridal township on train or by bus, as the case may be and it used to be an enviable fun all through the travelling when singing, shouting and eating, the marriage party would cover the distance, with bridal side making arrangements for refreshments on the way sides with ambience of hospitality peculiar to marriages. If it was reserved compartment of a railway train, the atmosphere of fun had to be different from what it used to be when the marriage party travelled by bus to cover the distance of thirty to forty miles. In such cases, on arrival at the bridal town, all the guests were made to stay at some huge place which was called 'Janwasa'. And that would become a picnic spot for all baratees who invented different modes for fun and entertainment. However, in case of local barat, 'Janwasa' would be a small place to accommodate close relations of bridegroom. Naturally, the kind of fun and leisure they had then is no longer available in today's marriages as it is becoming a normal practice to solemnize marriage mostly from bridegroom's hometown and bride's side agreeing to shift to the township of the bridegroom's family.

★ ★ ★

The whole family, including Jagan Babu, attended the marriage of Ramesh's daughter and by the time they returned it was almost midnight. They all went straight to their rooms and prepared to sleep. While Pushpaji took some time before she was snoring, Jagan Babu lay on the bed with his eyes wide open reflecting on the changing modes of organizing marriage functions. His mind went back to days in early fifties when he was a teenager and every celebration during the marriage of his cousin sister was pure fun for him.

Marriages those days were really fun filled full three days, not like today, a day's affair. His cousin sister's marriage, which he enjoyed immensely as a teenager, began with 'Roka ceremony' clubbed with 'Ring Ceremony' and 'Goadbharai' on the same day. Next important ceremony was 'Lagan' which involved invitation to guests on a massive feast, after 'Lagan' had been taken to bridegroom's home. Now, however, lagan is performed, may be with different names, but buffet is organized on contractual basis. But those days it would seem to have been hosted by the whole community with emotions dominating the scene. Food items were served on pattals and earthen saucers and water in earthen tumblers called kulhars to the guests sitting in rows over sheets on the ground. It was a sight to see when hundreds of guests were served by dozens of hospitable hands carrying can-made container called palla full of poories and kachauries, brought straight from the furnace and different items of food brought duly kept into specially carved out big serving utensils called chaukras and small buckets taken round insisting for more and more. Later, gradually this system of feasting got replaced by using crockery with cutlery for baratees sitting on chairs around tables placed in rows and then even this got replaced by buffet system involving self-service which is modern way of hosting feast. He recalled that on the first day reception of barat was organized with performance of 'Darwaza' for ceremonial welcome of bridegroom and baratees. Thereafter while guests were served with massive feast on the same pattern as it was on the occasion of Lagan, ceremony called Bhanwaren to solemnize wedding through Saptpadi was held in the enclosure of mandap. These rituals and ceremonies so far are common to all marriages including those held these days, but the difference between now and then starts from the second day when ceremonial feasts called 'Bhat' and 'Badhar' with specified items of food were served at lunch and dinner. In the afternoon of the same day a very interesting ceremony called 'Kunwar Kalewa' was held with lot of fanfare. The bridegroom was seated under the canopy of 'Mandap', surrounded by crowd of ladies representing relations and friends of the bride's family who were called upon, one by one, to honour the bridegroom with tilak on his forehead, followed by practically pushing a piece of sweetmeat in his already filled mouth, but not without some gift, in kind or cash. The ceremony would last for around couple of hours and he, with the mischievous lot, would watch and laugh at the bridegroom's plight with a sense of pity for unbearable tolerance of his belly. And the last and a very interesting ceremony which was held late in the evening after dinner on the second day and lasted almost till midnight was, 'Neotini'. The fun filled ceremony was held in a huge open field within the housing compound where both the parties gathered and were comfortable on ground, furnished with white sheets and pillows, facing each other and hosts sprinkling scent as a token of welcome. This was intended to be 'thanksgiving ceremony'. However, what began with sweet words of greetings, communicated formally with recitals of well composed verses, in Hindi and Urdu, in the name of 'Sehra' invariably turned into open forum for war of wits which culminated into verbal duels. But finally, the ceremony ended almost at midnight on pleasant note. On the third day, the curtain fell with the ritual called 'Vida'. The sight is the same now as it was then, bride crying with her family amongst tears of joy and people watching the scene with teary eyes amidst tunes of vida on dhol and baja.

It was almost midnight when he could slip into the lap of sleep.

"Dadu, nowadays many marriage portals and match making sites are available to pick and choose. How were marriages settled during your boyhood days," Rohan raised the question when Jagan Babu came for breakfast next morning. Ratna looked at him with red eyes, "Enough is enough, Rohan. Don't bother Papa any more by your unending questions."

But Rakhi, Rohan and Pinki who had picked up, in course of conversations, enough clues about the fun part of the marriages during their dadu's teenage days when marriages used to take atleast three days as against one day affair now, it was easy for them to conclude that settlement of marriages should also involve somewhat funny modes and methods.

"You see, there used to be then two ways for settling a marriage," Jagan Babu explained. "One, somebody known to the family, a relation or a friend or even an acquaintance, would suggest a suitable boy for the daughter of the other relation or vice-versa, vouching forcefully for the merits including the vocation, family status etc. After all other issues, including the give and take part, had been settled, venue would be fixed for seeing the girl, which normally had to be a public place like a park or a temple or any other similar place where boy's side would have a look at the girl and communicate the decision after consultations amongst family members. Quite often boys those days would leave the decision to elders in the family or say they were too shy and peevish to insist their willingness to see the girl."

"And what was the second mode?" asked Pinki with natural curiosity.

"Second mode of settlement was when some elderly relations gathered around cocktail table on some festive occasion and fixed the marriages of their children and grandchildren, in most of the cases, without giving much of a serious thought or leaving any scope for consultations by others in the family. None had the courage to stand up against the decision taken, right or wrong. And, once the word was out, there was no going back," Jagan Babu concluded.

"How funny! "Rohan cried and stopped short of commenting adversely.

"Yes, it was funny. But somehow the marriages worked," said Jagan Babu.

"I doubt," said Rakhi, "how can a thoughtless relationship forced on a family work successfully? How was it that the boys in question did not have powerful desire to see the girl with whom they were going to spend their entire life? It is understandable in case of girls who were supposedly the suppressed lot. But how could it be in case of boys," Rakhi spoke in unrestrained flow stung by the ludicrous aspect of settlement of marriages earlier.

Stirred by spontaneous reaction of Rakhi, Jagan Babu's mind slipped for a brief moment recalling with a smile an incident that proves million dollars worth of Rakhi's reaction. The incident related to the settlement of marriage of one of his cousin sisters.

The 'would- be- husband' was so curious and impatient to see his would-be-bride that he wore the look of a Rationing Inspector and knocked at bride's doors. The younger sister of the would-be-bride opened the door and, since she was a very pretty person, he went back, after asking some rationing related queries, happy at the thought of marrying the damsel of his dreams. He was shocked when he saw the bride after marriage but kept silent then. But when he shared his faux pas with his wife later, the story went round and became the joke of the year which was taken in a stride by him who shared the laughter with sly smiles.

"Sorry dadu for obstructing the flow," said Rakhi.

"It is ok, Rakhi. I will first respond to your reaction. As I explained earlier, we lived in large joint families with strict control of elders and authoritarian control of the head of the joint family. It was thus normal practice in most of the families for elders to select, choose and settle marriages of boys and girls in the family, rarely consulting the boy and seldom the girls. Many of the marriages were settled on cocktail and dinner tables of the elderly relations on occasions of festive gatherings and no one had the guts to challenge them for their decisions. You see, that was the reason that leaving aside a few families, headed by sensible elderly person, women were so cruelly dealt with and so unreasonably exploited that they practically languished with perpetual want and suffering and remained sick and hungry all through their lives." Jagan Babu poured out all the venom that had accumulated in his system since his childhood watching helplessly the plights of women around him.

While Rakhi marvelled at dadu's rational attitude, Rohan could not restrain himself. "Dadu, why they had to bear all this? Why could not the exploiters be dragged in the court and punished?"

"Rohan beta, we could not imagine to even think of what you are saying. The legal safeguards which now exist were nowhere in sight then. Hindu marriages were treated as a religious sacrosanct and were lived till the last breath of the spouses even when they were living hell."

"Were they all living like that, dadu?" asked Pinki innocently. She was trying to make two and two four.

"No, Pinki. There were very happy families as well," Jagan Babu tried to present a balanced picture. "Look, marriage has always been a gamble in India. If there is compatibility between wife and husband, if the family as a whole is decent, it goes on well; nothing more than occasional unavoidable tiffs. But if there is discord in the marriage and the family is mean and ruthless then the couple lives the life in hell. In some cases, husbands are victims alongwith their spouses and, in many cases, he is the piece of the villain, the master mind who upfronts his family in scheming worst atrocities leading to brides suicides and dowry deaths. The only difference between now and then is that there were a very few legal safeguards then and even those were beyond the reach of the common man. Unlike today, couples did not have the option to seek divorce and to live life of their choice. But gradually, as everything began to change, law began to take care of this aspect of our life and change became perceptible even in the attitudes of couples and their relations."

Rohan commented bluntly, "Dadu, that means our times are much better than the period of your childhood."

"Beta, it is not so simple. There has always been mix of good and bad in our lives and it will continue to be so at all times. I can dig hundreds of holes in today's ways of life. While legal provisions have gone a long way to safeguard the interests of young boys and girls, yet healthy conjugal life eludes many of them. Recourse to legal remedies entails problems of its own kind. Besides, legal safeguard itself is turning into a lethal weapon for exploitation in the hands of vicious minds. In ultimate analysis, it is the attitude that makes a difference," Jagan Babu said.

"Dadu, we see your point. It is not that everything has turn rosy," said Rakhi calmly.

"Well, it will fill volumes if we go on and on," Jagan Babu wanted to cut short the discussion. "I will only add that there is more of freedom for youths now than in our times. There are now so called love marriages, inter-caste marriages and even inter-communal marriages. Added to them, live-in relationships are coming in vogue. The cases of settled marriages are now on the wane. But there are more cases in courts for divorce, domestic violence, dowry deaths etc. Taking overall perspective in view, I believe that marriages are a matter of destiny and hence continues to be a gamble irrespective of barriers of time and boundaries," Jagan Babu said with a touch of finality and that was signal to call it a day. "Okay, enough for the day. Can I leave now?" He got up and walked towards his study room.

★ ★ ★

FUN AND FROLIC

Days rolled by and everyone in the family remained engaged in their respective routines. Gradually as the season changed and examinations of Rakhi, Rohan and Pinky were over, there was all pervading mood for enjoyment. To add spice, Jagan Babu's daughter Rashmi and son-in-law Shailendra intimated their programme to be with them during the vacations of their son, Pankaj and daughter, Sonakshi. And when they arrived, the entire atmosphere of the family changed from boring routine to spending time on innovating modes of fun. New dishes were tried, films were seen together, picnic was arranged and relations and friends frequented to meet Rashmi and Shailendra. There was no end to gossiping when all the grandchildren of Jagan Babu closeted themselves in a room.

In an atmosphere surcharged with mirth and gaiety, it was only natural to make the best of an auspicious occasion on coming Sunday, the birthday of Pinky, who was excited beyond measure. The whole week was spent in shopping. Cake was collected in the afternoon of Saturday and was kept ready with candles to be cut in the evening when Jagan Babu's brothers, sister and other family friends would gather. By then Pinky's friends had departed with their returned gifts.

And what followed on that auspicious day was an evening full of songs and dances with munching of sumptuous snacks and drinks of their choices. What made the evening a real musical treat was the songs sung by Jagan Babu and his brothers, Raman and Lucky. Since singing session moved rotationally, almost everyone had to sing, good, better or best, and those who could not sing danced hilariously to the tunes played on music system. Fun filled one liners thrown up by illustrious gathering turned the atmosphere boisterously mirthful.

The entire younger lot stayed there throughout and participated wholeheartedly. Surprisingly, they enjoyed songs sung by their dadus as picked up from the golden era of music, fifties, and sixties. Shailendra also proved to be a good singer. But Jagan Babu was the apple of everyone's eye because of his choice of songs and sweetness of his voice. He was known to have been capable of imitating top play back singers. He was particularly fond of ghazals and enjoyed imitating ghazals sung by Talat Mahmood, Mehdi Hassan, Ghulam Ali, Jagjit Singh. It was almost midnight when guests departed and gathering was dispersed.

Jagan Babu lay on his bed but sleep as usual deluded him. With his eyes wide open, he was enjoying the euphoria that engulfed him for his singing at the evening function. Recollection of different occasions when he made a mark as a singer in large and small gatherings since his childhood served to cheer him immensely.

When they were school going boys, he and his cousin of his age, who had equally sweet voice, were focal points for every one's attention because of their talent to imitate excellently hit songs of popular films. They occasionally travelled with his father and his colleagues of railways in Inter or second-class compartments between Moradabad and Bareilly, Uttar Pradesh and they were invariably asked to sing throughout the journey. He recalled how they sang in their effeminate voices, competing with each other the most melodious songs of films like Anarkali, Nagin, Baiju Bawra, Awara, Aah, Sri 420, Shabab, Deedar. He grew up singing at different venues and on different occasions, for different groups and audiences, on the lawns of college for friends, on farewells and during new year's celebrations. He participated in cultural programmes at training institute and at other workplaces, in musical concerts during festivals and family functions. Ironically, at the end of every session where he participated as singer he kept wondering if he really was a good singer. He could never bring himself to believe that he was a good singer. He realized gradually that he gained the name and popularity as a singer only because, somehow, he was catapulted into holding the mike and facing the gathering and that was how it began. That is how he ceased to be bathroom singer. And now while leading retired life he was basking in the glory of earned popularity as a singer and has developed guts to sing without hesitation unmindful of the response his tired voice evokes.

He did not know when he was overtaken by sleep.

Next day when they met for the lunch Rakhi said with genuine admiration, "My God, dadu! How sweet is your voice! I realized it when I heard you seriously yesterday. None of us has been lucky enough to inherit your talent," she bemoaned.

"Dadu, how did you develop your talent for singing?" asked Pinky impatiently.

"Pinki, unlike today, we did not have the facility then to hear songs of our choices on YouTube, transistors, televisions and such other gadgets," Jagan Babu responded to Pinki's query. "Since I did not have the means to hear songs of my choice at home, I would walk miles in slow motion following rickshaws and horse driven carts called tangas fitted with loud speakers and films display boards, just to enjoy the sweetness of the songs of films like Baiju Bawra, Anarkali, Nagin, Awara, Sri 420, played aloud to attract attention of the people to the films in cinema halls. Besides, playing popular films songs on loud speakers was the only mode of creating festive atmosphere on auspicious occasions and family ceremonies in the locality and, believe me, I would put aside what I was studying, even if that required serious involvement, and lend my ears to the song of my choice, noting down hurriedly their lyrics like the one 'O duniya ke rakhwale....' sung so melodiously by Mohmmad Rafi in the film Baiju Bawra."

He stopped for a while and then said, "Well, I have been a typical bathroom singer with penchant to copy the masters. Yes, once the sweetness of a tune stuck to my ears, I couldn't rest till I was able to imitate it. It was immaterial that the song was new or old. It should be sweet enough to appeal to my ears."

Left alone in his study room where he went to relax after lunch on his long chair it was natural for him to be nostalgic about his abundant love for music and passion for singing.

He felt grateful to Almighty for whatever little talent of music he has in him. He reflected that singing, like any other fine art, is a divine gift. Sachin Tendulkar, even if he so desired, could never be a play back singer and these great singers could never be cricketers par excellence even if they wanted to be. He considered himself lucky to inherit his love for music from his father's fondness for music. He recalled with a streak of strange pleasure his childhood when he would habitually jump to his father's bed every morning and heard him singing in his sweet voice classical songs of his choice. He distinctly remembers a line of a song his father used to recite almost every morning 'dekho re ek bala jogi dware pe mere ayo hai re' in the tune of raga Bhairvi. He could not help laughing at his madness for music as he recalled how he would invariably stop at the screen side of the film theatre Raj Hans on his way back home from his school and would lend his ears too close to the wall on the screen side just to hear and enjoy the snake charming tune on instrument called 'Been' in the film Nagin. He had seen the film twice stealthily earlier. He loved the tune so much that he mastered it on harmonium. He smiled while remembering the day when, in early fifties, his friend's parents in adjoining house purchased newly introduced Murphy Radio and he, alongwith his cousins and friends, would unhesitatingly rush to his friend's house and would sit with their ears to songs from Binaca Geet Mala, a very popular programme then, relayed from Ceylon Radio Station. The mesmerizing voice of its most popular announcer, Ameen Sayani, still rings in his ears as if he was sitting by the side of the radio. Later, when portable transistor radio came on the scene and became versatile companion, knowledge enhancer and repository of film songs, he began to enjoy entertaining programmes of Vivid Bharti Service of All India Radio. My God, how time has drastically changed gradually in the past seven decades, he wondered. Now we have Google, YouTube, Alexa to provide lyrics and have Smart Phone or ipad to relay songs just by pressing the button repeatedly until we are able to copy a song with meticulous accuracy in terms of lyrics and tunes. But in those days, printed booklets were the only source for lyrics of films' songs. The easy way out then was to chase the song at the source of its relay for noting down the lyrics and that is what he used to do with meticulous care to be accurate once a song stuck to his mind. He remembered to have spent many restless days and nights in imitating the rendering of a song by repeatedly rehearsing it in his own voice. It is now height of technical advancement when anyone who can sing can have the songs of his/her choice recorded in his/her voice with music and lyrics of the original song, thanks to availability of karaoke on YouTube and applications like Star Maker on smart mobile phones.

A few weeks later Jagan Babu had just returned from somewhere and had settled on the sofa in the drawing room when he found the music system blaring with a loud song from some latest movie, accompanied by the sound of rhythmic steps, coming from adjoining room. With no intention to mar the pleasure of his grandchildren, he wanted somehow volume to be reduced only. He began to fiddle with his ears so that he could shut them to the loud shrill music he was finding difficult to withstand. But Ratna, his daughter-in-law, who, while passing through the drawing room to the kitchen, found Jagan Babu restlessly rubbing his ears, instinctively retreated to the adjoining room and switched off the music system. What followed was the eerie of sudden silence and Ratna watched with a smile Jagan Babu returning to his natural ease. Irked by sudden fall of silence, Pinky, who was dancing to the tune of her choice, came running to see what went wrong with the system and, finding the switch off, was about to run towards kitchen to shout in protest at her mummy, but stopped short abruptly when she saw dadu sitting on sofa. In quick steps, she made a hasty retreat to her study room.

Jagan Babu was careful enough not to hurt the sensibilities of his children by criticizing them for their taste of the music which naturally was at variance with the taste of his own. He knew it was an inevitable generational conflict which was visible in every aspect of living from sense of dressing to sense of behaving with others.

He knew it for certain that they did not like old songs at all. He was happy to see them all living in their islands as he lived in his own. But the conflict invariably became sharp because while Jagan Babu loved to hear the songs mostly from the golden era of fifties and sixties, his grandchildren dismissed the songs and films of that era utterly slow, old and boring.

It was not that Jagan Babu was averse to the music his children loved and liked to hear. What annoyed him was their refusal to be open minded on the subject. But he was not ready to lose his ground and looked for an opportunity when he could clear his perspective before them. And the opportunity came up soon one day when all of them got up and settled in the drawing room before dinner after having watched a music programme on television.

And what they had watched together was 'Sa Re Ga Ma Pa, Little Champs' a music programme specifically designed by enlisting the budding talents amongst boys and girls in their teens, and surprisingly, presenting even as young as five year olds who were seen singing with ease and felicity of master singers. The programme had begun with the anchor floating on the floor of the performing area pouring out welcoming words torrentially while camera moved slowly to capture faces of three prominent personalities of music world occupying seats as judges and a wide range of talents in the field of music forming the jury. The participating children were seated decorously in an enclosure and were invited one after the other, punctuated by evaluations and commentary on quality of their performances. To add spice, the anchor played pranks in between making the entire studio bursting with laughter. Luckily, on that day, famous music director, Pyare Lal of Laxmikant Pyarelal fame, alongwith his wife, was the guest of honour whose opinion was sought after every performance by the male and female child artiste.

Interestingly, in different episodes of the serial the child artistes would usually sing songs picked up from playback singers of the golden era as well as present day artistes which broadly included Lata Mangeshkar, Asha Bhosle, Geeta Dutt, Shamshad Begum, Mohammed Rafi, Talat Mehmood, Manna Dey, Kishore Kumar, Hemant Kumar, Mahendra Kapoor, Kumar Sanu, Udit Narain, Sonu Nigam, Shaan, Arijit Singh, Shreya Ghoshal, Alka Yagnik, Neha Kakkar, Sunidhi Chauhan, Anuradha Paudwal and many other prominent singers and music directors. That day the entire family of Jagan Babu heard the little champs with rapt attention, the songs largely composed by Lakshmikant Pyare Lal, between peals of laughter incited by clown like gimmicks of the anchor.

Once the programme was over, all of them shifted to drawing room and Ratna moved to kitchen where the maid was preparing for the dinner. While waiting to be called on dining table, Jagan Babu teasingly provoked his grandchildren to react since they had watched the programme seriously without giving impression of being bored at any stage at all.

"Yes dadu, It was really mesmerizing to hear children so young singing with such perfection popular songs sung by top playback singers," Rakhi was first to comment.

"I am glad, Rakhi, that since most of the songs sung by little champs were old enough for you as composed by Laxmi Kant Pyarelal, I am surprised that you nevertheless liked them," commented Jagan Babu.

But Rohan said just for the sake of saying something perhaps to make his stand clear on the subject, "Dadu, I cannot put up with slow songs and slow music. I do not have the patience," said Rohan.

'Good, Rohan. I admire your frankness. But tell me whether you enjoyed the songs by these talented children in today's programme," enquired Jagan Babu.

"Yes, dadu. We did enjoy most of the songs sung by the boys and girls," replied Rohan hesitatingly. He was seemingly reluctant to concede against what was so deeply entrenched into his growing mind.

And then Jagan Babu turned his attention to his real target, Pinky, who missed no opportunity to mock at old songs calling them slow and boring and that too in the presence of her dadu. Pinky was sitting silent. In fact, as the most vociferous critic of old songs, she was caught in a dilemma. But she was quick to recover from the moment of embarrassment.

"Yes dadu, I liked the children of that delicate age singing with such confidence. And I liked because songs were really sweet," replied Pinky with unexpected frankness.

"I am happy, Pinky, that you have shown liking for good songs irrespective of the fact whether they were new or old. You see, music is not bound by any barriers of time. And that is the point that I have always tried to make. There is nothing like an old song or a new song. It is either a good song, sweet and melodious, or a bad song, dull and boring. It cannot be liked or disliked on the plea of old or new." Jagan Babu paused for a second to watch the reaction and found all of them, including Ravindra and Ratna, listening to him with interest.

'But dadu, it is the percentage that matters," said Rakhi.

"Well, Rakhi beta, that will involve market surveys purely from commercial angle whereas what we are discussing is nothing but only sweetness which should be the sole test for judging a song or a tune of music, as far as we are concerned," replied Jagan Babu.

He continued even while moving towards dining table where dinner was being arranged. "Not everyone is born with soft ears for music. To many, music is fun when it is loud and hitting while for persons like me music is something that goes to the heart through ears. And I am not specifying any particular type of music. It could be classical music, film's music or folk songs or even English songs and for that matter, in any language. My only condition is that it should be sweet and sonorous and should appeal to the ears as such. To me a good song or a tune is like flow of a spring with rhythmic sound that soothes the listener and not like tumultuous tides of an ocean which threaten to hit the ear drums."

While dinner was served on the table, none seemed to break the chain of interesting conversation. Even while munching their meals all the three of his grandchildren kept raising one question after the other until Ratna intervened saying that they should let Papa have his meals.

But in the afternoon while they sat together for tea and refreshment, Pinky could not contain her curiosity and asked abruptly, "Dadu, who is your favourite playback singer?"

'It is a difficult question for me to answer. The reason is that the period of music that I talked about as golden was so because during those around two decades, starting from late forties, we had the best of the talents, both amongst male and female singers. It is difficult for me to pinpoint single one as my favourite. They were all my favourites for their unique styles and sweetness of their voices," Jagan Babu seemed quite clear on this issue.

"Still, dadu, there must be someone whom you consider the best," added Rohan.

"Not exactly I will say best, because everyone was best in terms of his and her own styles and voices. If you are really keen to know about the singer whose voice I like most, I will explain why it is difficult for me to name a single singer. It will take time. Can we talk about it any other day?" said Jagan Babu.

"No dadu, no," cried Rohan. "We are keen to know all about music of your time. We cannot leave it to any other time. Please dadu."

"Alright! The names of great singers of my times are: Mohammed Rafi, Hemant Kumar, Talat Mahmood, Kishore Kumar, Manna Dey, Mahendra Kapoor, Bhupendra. Have you heard their names?"

"What are you saying, Dadu? We listen to their songs on television and transistor. We keep hearing if I like the song and shift to other channels if don't. I know the names of female playback singers who are famous, and they are: Lata Mangeshkar, Asha Bhosle, Geeta Dutt, Shamshad Begum. Am I correct, dadu," said Pinky.

Rakhi, who was listening to the conversation with an academic interest, applauded Pinky loudly for her general knowledge which made every one laugh aloud. "And dadu, we also hear songs of Sonu Nigam, Kumar Sanu, Shaan, Udit Narain, Arjit Singh and also female singers like Alka Yagnik, Shreya Ghoshal, Neha Kakkar, Sunidhi Chauhan, Kavita Krishnamurthy, Anuradha Paudwal. I read and heard a lot about the contribution of some of the music directors of your time for having composed the best of the songs. We know about those who are popular in our times. Let us know about them, dadu," Rakhi requested Jagan Babu to talk about music directors.

"Naushad Ali, Shankar-Jaikishan, C. Ramchandra, S.D. Burman, R. D Burman, Laxmikant- Pyarelal, O.P. Nayyer, Madan Mohan, Khayyam, Roshan, Hemant Kumar, Salil Choudhury are the names of some of the most talented music directors of fifties and sixties. They, in coordination with top lyricist and composers of the period like Sahir Ludhianvi, Shakeel Badayuni, Kaifi Azmi, Shailendra, Mujrooh Sultanpuri, Anand Bakshi, Nida Fazli, Jaidev and Javed Akhtar, Gulzar, Gopaldas Niraj composed songs which will continue to be heard till eternity. Beti, that period was a phenomenon when the deadly combination of superb lyricists, play back singers and music composers and directors created songs and musical tunes which reverberate all over the world breaking barriers of time and borders."

"Dadu, I am sorry to bother you. But my original question is still unanswered. Who is your pet singer?" Pinky repeated her question.

"Well, each one of the singers of my time had a few or more songs to their credit which have stamp of their peculiarity and are known and heard even now because of that peculiarity of their voices and their styles combined. But amongst them, Mohammed Rafi has been the one who obsessed me with his golden voice and for its versatility. While, in his early years, he sang songs whose superb melody keeps ringing in my ears even now like those in the films Baiju Bawra, Udan Khatola, Deedar, Amar, Aan, he sang with equal ease and melody hilarious songs for actors like Shammi Kapoor, Joy Mukherji and the likes as in the films Junglee and Phir Wahi Dil Laya Hoon, Love in Tokyo and so on. His songs have the appeal for people of all ages. To repeat it, one thing that makes Mohammed Rafi very popular and considered by many as all-time best is because of his versatility and adaptability which no one else could match even to this day. If on the one hand he sang superb quality songs with classical music as their base as in films Baiju Bawra, he was equally comfortable singing songs like 'Champi, Tel Malish', 'Jane Khan Mera Jigar Gaya ji', 'Ajhoon Na Aye Balma' for comedians like Johnny Walker and Mehmood and even pathetic songs for the beggars on street like the song 'Tumhare Hain Tum Se Daya Maang te Hain'. He was master in moulding his voice to suit the character on the screen, be it Dilip Kumar or Devanand or Raj Kapoor or Shammai Kapoor or Joy Mukherjee, or Johnny walker or Mehmood, and that kind of versatility no other playback singer could display. He is the most liked, loved and imitated singer and nobody could match his popularity as a singer. And above all, he was a great human being, modest and down to earth," Jagan Babu spoke in a single breath.

"Who else, dadu?" enquired Pinki

"So, I do not have to repeat that I love Rafi Sahib's voice. But there were others very talented singers and I love their songs for their unique sweetness, for their own types of songs and music with their prominently distinguishable voices. Each one has been a singer in his own right not only for the sweetness but also for unique flavour in their singing style".

"What do you mean, dadu, by uniqueness of style?" Interrupted Rakhi

"Take the example of singer Talat Mahmood's voice which is unique in its own way. I find it sweet as a flow of a spring and I love his style of singing that suited his velvety voice. He sang songs mostly in the format of ghazals. Then I am also madly in love with the voice of Manna Dey and his unique style of singing. His songs with classical touch always have a mesmerising effect on me. I just get lost in them. Mohammed Rafi was reported to have commented that while the whole world heard him, he used to listen to Manna Dey. Then the great singer Mukesh, whose nasal sweet voice is very unique, has given many memorable songs. Similarly, the voice and unique style of singing of grand music composer cum playback singer Hemant Kumar is enchanting in its own way. Kishore Kumar is sweet and unique, inimitable, and playful, and yet most tried for imitation. As for female singers, the more said about Lata Mangeshkar and her sister Asha Bhosle is far less and not enough. They have dominated the scene with their very sweet voices distinguished by their differing styles. There have been other female play back singers like Noor Jehan, Suraiya, Geeta Dutt, Shamshad Begum, Suman Kalyanpur, Mubarak Begum, Uma Devi who won the hearts of millions by their unique styles and velvety voices. Noor Jehan who shifted to Pakistan after partition was the most revered female singer who was on scene prior to Lata Mangeshkar and occupied top space in film industry. And the beauty was that instead of being oddly competitive, they were each other's admirers. Will you believe me that Lataji, even after having reached the pinnacle, had the regard for Noor Jehan as her elder sister," Jagan Babu nodded towards Rakhi to ensure that she was satisfied with the reply.

"Amongst modern singers who is the one you like most?" asked Rakhi.

"To be very frank, somehow, I don't possess the same intimate grasp about modern films and their music. While I know the names of many singers whose voice I like but, in many cases, I fail to recognize voices accurately and distinguish them from others. While I enjoy a voice when I hear, I cannot place it. You can call it generational gap. I like the voices of Sonu Nigam, Kumar Sanu, Shaan, Udit Narain, Arjit Singh, Sukhwinder Singh and also female singers like Kavita Krishnamurthy, Alka Yagnik, Shreya Ghoshal, Sunidhi Chauhan, Neha Kakkar, Anuradha Paudwal. They are all very good singers. some other famous names of music world are A.R Rehman, Bappi Lahiri, Anu Malik, Vishal Bhardwaj, Anil Biswas, Himesh Reshammiya. But right from the beginning I liked Jagjit Singh, Mehdi Hassan and Ghulam Ali," replied Jagan Babu.

"Mehdi Hassan and Ghulam Ali were the Pakistani Singers," reminded Pinki.

"So what? Music has no boundaries. I think it is enough for a day," Jagan Babu declared and walked towards his study room to relax on his long chair.

★ ★ ★

After dinner while everybody withdrew straight to their rooms, Jagan Babu returned to his bedroom after a brief round of walk and lied down on his bed and tried to sleep which as usual evaded him. While Pushpaji was preparing to sleep, Jagan Babu sat on his bed with pillow on his back and began to fiddle with television in the hope to catch up with something interesting to hold him till he felt sleepy. There were good films on different channels like 3 Idiots, Baghban, Bulandi, Tridev, Dil Wale Dulhania Le jayein Ge, Veer Zara, but they, being repeats of number of times, did not interest him. He put the remote aside on side table and lied down with eyes closed and was soon drifted in the past.

He found himself as a teenager standing in the unmanageable queue of crowded booking window of Jagat Talkies in his hometown Bareilly unmindful of scorching heat to buy two tickets for the film Uran Khatola. Together with his pal cousin, he had collected in hush hush atmosphere of mid hot day empty bottles and old newspapers, when all family members were asleep after lunch, jumped out from the backyard and rushed to the scrap dealer to sell the collected material. They got enough to buy two tickets, each for ten annas and something, and were now sweating at the booking window. It was a day show and hence they could be back before people at home got out of their rooms. There were five film theatres in the town then. That is how he could see films then. And now he has only to surf with his remote to choose a film to enjoy it in the comfort of his bedroom at his convenience. Theatres were there in Delhi earlier but now they have vanished with the coming up of concept of mall with multiplex. He is blamed by his grandchildren for being biased in favour of films produced in fifties and sixties and called that period the golden era of films and music. They refuse to see the fact that good films thereafter came only by chance because films began to be churned out at a speed faster than rolls of fabrics in textile mill. They also refuse to accept that there is nothing like old film or a new film. There is either a good film or a bad film. A good film, irrespective of its period of production, is the one which is well made in terms of direction and acting and is thematically entertaining and meaningful. It is generation gap. They will understand as they will grow further that cinema presents on the screen the replication of life as it exists on earth with multifarious facets and hence has become a powerful mirror for the society. It is unfortunate that somehow rubbish films are minting money to the tune of hundred crores and that people hail a mediocre film because it is touching hundred crores. The fast speed at which films are made to make money at the box office has not only led to considerable decline in the production of good films in terms of percentage but also has also caused scarcity of ideas. Poverty of thought has forced the tendency to churn out remakes of films which were hit at the box office like Shah Rukh Khan's 'Don', J.P. Dutta's 'Umrao Jaan', Ram Gopal Verma's 'Sholey' and the process goes on.

Finding him awake and restless with television on Pushpa got up, switched off the television, and said in semi-sleep condition, "Why don't you sleep? Are you alright?"

He replied, "Yes, I am Okay. You know it takes some time before I get to sleep."

And he seriously made efforts to be taken by sleep. But while Pushpa was fast asleep, Jagan Babu kept struggling to induce sleep and, in the process, found himself again hooked to the trail of thought he left a few minutes ago.

He smiled at the thought that if his grandchildren came to know that even today, he has liking for B/W films although they are now a thing of the past, he would become butt of joke. But this is something which is difficult for them to understand. He recalled that when he watched films then, even if they were B/W, he enjoyed them immensely because screen in a film theatre was the dividing line beyond which existed quite a different world of a film for those watching it sitting on this side of the screen. That was the reason that the scenes like dream sequence created in films like Awara, used to transform the viewers to quite a different world than the matter- of-fact world we live in. The actors of screen were looked by the viewers 'the stuff dreams are made of' as if they belonged to the other world, not like the men and women of flesh and blood. With the introduction of colour films, the screen that divided the world into two withered away merging two different worlds into one and the distinction between the viewers and the screen actors vanished. And with this has gone the euphoria created by magic of films. And that reminded him a small incident. When he was student in Moradabad, he could see from a vantage point while returning from school the veteran actor Prithivi Raj Kapoor, with white shawl round his broad shoulders, climbing the staircases of Raj Hans theatre, accompanied by his youngest son, Shashi Kapoor, a teenager then. A huge crowd was there and, as he looked at him from a distance, he felt as if a demi- god has descended from the heaven on earth. And gradually as he grew and with him the world grew and changed, he had many occasions to see the film stars at the shooting sites and even met some of them in course of his trips to Bombay and he found that the euphoria he lived earlier was no longer there. It began to evaporate as the two different worlds began to merge and films assumed a realistic posture gradually as against wholesome dreamy character they possessed earlier. He knew that what he felt might not be true about others, but even now he was capable of enjoying a B/W film of yesteryears provided it has strong storyline, treated sensibly with good acting, sweet and enchanting music and high production quality from the standard of even those times. Situation is quite different now when actors appear regularly on different fora to promote their films.

He did not know when sleep overtook him and soon he was snoring aloud.

TUG OF WAR

It was Sunday. Jagan Babu was lying in a thoughtful mood on his long chair in the drawing room reflecting philosophically how two minor incidents proved to be turning points in his career and consequentially impacted his life.

He knew always he was a mediocre student and yet he could earn the covetous title of being a brilliant person or say, he was catapulted into being considered so. He was good in other subjects, no doubt, and was certainly excellent in English, but was very poor in mathematics. And therefore, there was no end to his jubilation when he learnt that mathematics was not a compulsory subject for the High school examination. Ironically, therefore, he passed high school in the year 1953 with science but without Mathematics as his subject. But since he had nurtured the ambition to be a medical practitioner, the profession that he held at a pedestal of divinity, he took admission in class Eleventh where, despite science having been his subject, he couldn't do without basic understanding of mathematics. Every word that the lecturer spoke fell on his deaf ears. One of his cousins, who was with him in the same class, noticed it and lost no time in reporting it to his father who arranged for his shifting to Arts side as it was just the beginning of the session. And there went smashing his dream to be a medical practitioner. That was the period when his father expired, and with his mind affected badly by the tragedy, he could not succeed that year. Perhaps his performance graph would have been sliding down but for a caustic remark of his grand uncle which proved to be a turning point for his career. As he entered the room where his aunt was preparing for school examination, she sought his guidance on some point of her English lesson. But before he could even begin to explain it to her, granduncle, in whose affectionate patronage he had grown so far, was heard telling her in his caustic tone, "Why are you asking him? Had he studied enough laboriously, he wouldn't have failed." His remark hit him like sharp edge of an arrow. Tears trickled down his eyes. That moment onward, he put his heart and soul into his studies, scored very good rankings subsequently in his studies and gradually earned the reputation of being brilliant student with prospects of a shining career. But for this turning point, he would have been languishing as a good for nothing fellow.

"Namaste Tauji", suddenness of Ranbir's voice broke the chain of this thought. He lifted his head and found his nephew, Ranbir and brother Raman walking in with his wife, Sushma alongwith Bimla and Sunita, wives of his nephews. His grandniece Vinita and grandnephews Naveen and Runchit were the last to enter.

"Come, come, Arey Wah, what a surprise!" Jagan Babu spoke aloud in his typical style. He looked around and enquired, "Where is Nitin?"

"Nitin had to go to his office today for some urgent work. He may come directly from the office," replied Raman.

Before Naveen, Vinita and Runchit could make a move to go in, Rakhi, Rohan and Pinky came running in the drawing room on hearing the familiar voices of their granduncle and uncle. Since their childhood, they have been fascinated by the company of their uncles who were known for their sparkling wit with sweet mix of humour. They had grown together playing pranks with their cousins Naveen, Vinita and Ruchit.

"It will be a great fun today as Lucky will also be coming," Raman announced as a breaking news. "Look, they are entering."

Jagan Babu, who loved being with his family and friends, had a broad smile on his face as Lucky touched his feet followed by Samarth. Sonam and Samarth sat close to their brothers and sisters and Sushma, Subhadra and Nirmila went towards kitchen where Ratna had gone inside to instruct the maid to serve tea and snacks in the drawing room and to brief her about the menu for lunch. They soon returned in the hall to come and go again and again, turn by turn, to check the progress in the kitchen.

Normally the youngsters would go inside to have fun in their own ways, but that day they stayed back.

Raman dragged a chair close to where Jagan Babu was sitting on his long chair and said in a conspiratorial tone as if it was a subject of immense value of national interest, though he broached it just to say something for the sake of saying something, "Bhai Sahib, last evening when the film Devdas, produced and directed by Sanjay Leela Bhansali, was telecast I watched it seriously because Ranbir and Nitin had praised a lot. They had seen it when it was released in theatres. I really felt bad because the literary worth of the film was completely overshadowed by the glamour of the sets and uncalled for compromises, a clear-cut deviation from the original novel."

The film with Shah Rukh Khan playing the title role opposite Aishwarya Rai and Madhuri Dixit was hit at the box office. Raman's statement triggered quite a debate on the subject of films in general and the whole lot was now divided into two camps. It was now a tug of war between two generations.

Jagan Babu, who had seen the film earlier, intervened to say that the latest version of Devdas would naturally appeal to most of the viewers because they saw it as an excellent piece of entertainment, full of fun and glamour.

"Let us be clear about one thing," he said. "Most of the people go to see a film purely for entertainment and they judge it primarily for its entertainment value. But since I have read the novel by the same name written by Sharad Chandra Chattopadhyay and have seen almost all the popular versions of film based on the novel, I will not look to it as a mere piece of entertainment. I expect the film to necessarily abide by the plot of the original literary work with the same ambience, to the extent possible, as it exists there in the novel. But to all those who have not read the novel, it is as good or bad as any other new film. Anyway, there is no point in stretching arguments on the subject and wasting your time."

Raman nodded in agreement and added with a pinch of salt, "Thanks to mobile and SMS culture picking up, there is over all deterioration in the taste of people."

"Yes, you are right," said Jagan Babu. "So far as films are concerned, it is one thing to like a film and quite another to appreciate it. A viewer is able to appreciate a good film directly in proportion to the quantum of intelligence he is able to apply to match it with level of intelligence involved in creating that film. Barring exceptions, most of the films cater to popular taste, from laughter to tears. Let us not forget that films are produced largely to succeed at the box office."

Of all the younger lot, which was hearing the comments silently, Naveen made bold to speak out, "But Tauji, most of us have that level of intelligence to understand films properly. But we just do not have the patience as most of the earlier films were normally slow and boring."

"Yes, normally. I agree with Naveen," Jagan Babu dismissed the whole discussion as irrelevant. He said, "I agree that the pace of films earlier was normally not fast for want of technological advancement. The production tools like camera were not as advanced as they are now. Films in the theatres, in big or small towns, were the only effective and easily accessible source of entertainment then for entertainment hungry population. But film production at that time was not that easy a job as it is now. You see, the whole film production team, from script writer to photographer, editor and director had to meddle for months with traditional tools to come up with final print ready to be screened in cinema halls. Naturally, while producers tried every gimmick to attract viewers, people had to accept whatever was offered to them. Now, the entire production process has undergone complete transformation. It is natural for today's generation to laugh at the short comings because of all kinds of handicaps which existed at that point of time. But lack of advance technological support was duly compensated at that time by hard work of the production teams."

Pinki jumped up with her own comments. "My God, how ridiculous the old black and while films were with heroine singing in the fields around trees!" she said mockingly.

"Yes, it is true that many of the earlier films had that peculiar trend of hero-heroine singing in the green fields around the trees. But the fact is that common man then and even now like to see dance and music on screen and film makers cater to their taste. To say it differently, for a common viewer then as it is now X film was as good as film Y, because they visit the picture halls for enjoying a film without bothering their heads on issues relating to thematic excellence or cinematographic values of films. Any single factor like story, music or comedy could be the reason for the viewer to enjoy the film. And that was how many films celebrated silver jubilee or even more of weeks in every town. All the same, I can say with certainty that every year a few films were so brilliantly made that their excellence transcended the barriers of boundaries as well as of time. To appreciate a film, one has to have an open mind," Raman spoke incessantly in an effort to wipe out the prejudicial approach adopted by most of the youngsters.

"Say whatever dadu, but it is difficult for us to see old films which are slow and boring," Pinky insisted stubbornly.

"Well, if you shut your mind and refuse to entertain fresh ideas, that is your choice," retorted Jagan Babu. "If you do not want to know the reason why some of the well-made films are slow in pace, that is your problem. You should understand that the pace of a film is determined by the requirements of the plot and its final quality depends on the skill of the director whose efforts can take it to lofty heights or make a mess of it by poor handling. Then there are many contributory factors like choice of cast, quality of music and so on. We should also not ignore the limitations of a period in terms of use of technology and facilities for shooting."

"Pinky, if you see, for instance, film 'Kanoon' produced by B. R. Chopra, you cannot take your eyes off screen and will sit for the entire duration of two and a half hours on the edge of the chair," sudden rejoinder came from Nalin who was hearing silently when Jagan Babu and Raman were talking. "And for you it is a very old film. It was produced in 1960. There were many brilliant films produced in Fifties and sixties. I remember films like Awara, Anarkali, Baiju Bawra, Nagin were in cinema halls celebrating silver and golden jubilees and we had seen them number of times for their entertainment value with superb music."

There was call for lunch and all of them moved towards dining table. After lunch was over, while Raman and Lucky with their families said goodbye and were seen off, all others returned to their rooms.

★ ★ ★

Jagan Babu stretched his legs on his bed for after- lunch nap. But since his mind was in perpetual grip of inferiority complex about being poor in mathematics, he found himself reflecting on it once again as soon as he closed his eyes. He, however, recalled with smile this time how God came to his rescue when he was in the midst an awkward situation only because of this handicap. He heaved a sigh of relief when he was mysteriously out of it.

He recalled with a touch of self-pity, though with a smile at this stage, how he had felt a mountain of weight removed from his head when he learnt that mathematics was not a compulsory subject for the High school examination conducted by Uttar Pradesh Board, Allahabad. Naturally, he passed high school in the year 1953 without mathematics as his subject. He could not help laughing at the irony later on how mathematics was made optional for only couple of years, as if only to render him handicapped for the rest of his life. It pinched him seriously when he was assigned by his cousin brother the task of coaching his pupil of class viii, the son and the daughter of a senior police functionary, at their residence for about a week because he had to be out of station. He was told to skip mathematics and take up other subjects. One of those seven days when he entered the residence in the civil lines, he found the father of the pupil sitting in the lawn meddling on something with a pen and a notebook. The moment he stepped in the gate with his bicycle, the father called him and as soon as he settled down on the chair by his side, he asked him to help him solve an arithmetic problem which he had been toiling to solve. And then while he kept explaining the problem in mathematical terms, each word spoken by him was falling on his deaf ears. He felt his head being hammered by a stick. He pretended trying to understand the problem, but since it was going blank on his wooden head, he kept praying silently to God to come to his rescue and save him from his predicament. And look, the Almighty seemed moved by his prayer and sent the messengers to rescue him. A police Jeep stopped at the gate and a group of police personnel got down and walked towards them. Seeing them coming towards him, the father deferred the exercise to be taken up some other time. And that 'some other time' never came for him again as he was relieved of the responsibility on return of his cousin in a couple of days .

SCREAMING AT SCREEN

It was a warm summer day. Jagan Babu, after having shuffled the pages of newspaper, was now fiddling with T.V. remote to open a news channel that could give the roundup of national and international news.

That was the stage when Shamsher Singh, Alekh Sharma and Mahesh Goyal, who had retired from the same service as Jagan Babu, landed there with their families. While their wives Gayatri, Prabha, and Neena and their daughters-in-law went straight inside and joined Pushpa Devi and Ratna, their grown up sons Narendra, Arjun, Shantanu, Somesh, Adhir and Sudhir stayed there. Rakhi, Rohan, and Pinki did move in for a while but returned in the drawing room to enjoy the firework that was to ensue.

"What is going on, Jagan?" spoke Shamsher even before he had fully settled down there. He was temperamentally a carefree man who took things in his stride rather than bemoaning for what he missed at his age, things of the past, which most of the people of his age thought were always much better than what they are now.

"Nothing Shamsher. I was trying to catch up with the news on television," replied Jagan Babu with a touch of irritation. "While I kept changing channels, one after the other, I could not find a single one where I could stop and focuss. What I find is news ticker running below the main screen on a moving belt, overshadowed by loud dominating advertising visuals. Headlines ran fleeting too fast to be caught by the eyes."

"What is there surprising, Jagan?" Intervened Alekh Sharma. "When there are more than hundred channels, each competing with others to gain TRP, for all the twenty four hours and, for all the seven days, you have to have news on the screen presented differently by each channel."

"But it is highly irritating to see things in such a mess," Jagan Babu said irritably.

Even after lapse of decades, Jagan Babu continued to live in his old frame of mind when there used to be scheduled news bulletins of ten to fifteen minutes durations at fixed timings of the day on two channels of Doordarshan, capturing the goings on all over the world effectively in nutshell. Shamsher, Alekh and Goyal, somehow, learnt to pick news from any channel without fuss and even watched debates just for enjoying 'Cock fights'.

"Please take tea with hot Pasta and Pakoras and your irritation will vanish, I guarantee," Ratna announced while entering the drawing room with tea and snacks. She was accompanied by Gayatri, Prabha and Neena. But the interruption did not have any disturbing impact on the tempo of discussion.

"Yes, we really need tea," Mahesh Goyal remarked with a smile, "Jagan Bhai, why should we be irritated, when, in some way, we were part of the changing scenario? You see, technology opened up opportunities with mind boggling innovations and the world shrunk into a global village. It was natural for us to be impacted by other countries and for things to change."

"Yes, I agree," Jagan Babu said thoughtfully. "With more than hundred channels telecasting programmes as long as TRP supports them with 'to hell with the people' approach, what else can we expect? News telecast at times depended for material on fictional characters as picked up from serials, while Serials keep dragging indefinitely testing patience of the viewers to withstand make believe gimmicks and unexpected improbabilities."

"By now we should be accustomed to the changed pattern of living because we cannot turn the clock back. Besides, why should we assume that all that has come to stay as changed is bad as compared to their previous existence?" Mahesh Goyal cleared his perspective on the issue.

"And all this change has occurred as a result of fast advancing technology. That is good. I have nothing against it. I am annoyed at human failure to keep the tiger in control. We have mounted a tiger but, later or sooner, we will find it difficult to unmount it and that can result in disaster. Coming generations will have to pay a heavy price for our failure in taming the tiger that technology is," The bubble busted after all.

"Uncle, sorry for interruption," interjected Narendra, "What is wrong if there are hundreds of television channels? We should be happy to have variety of news, views and other programmes from so many private channels instead of being fed by a couple of Government controlled channels as was the position earlier."

Jagan Babu responded calmly to Narendra's comment, "Narendra, what I see emerging is a phenomenon where multiple television channels with their telecasting potential are becoming easy tools of vicious propaganda in the hands of irresponsible greedy people and parties who could shell out huge amounts to purchase news and views. My point is that these channels should not be instrumental in churning out fake news. If that happens credibility of the entire media will erode."

As if suddenly reminded of something of importance Shamsher Singh intervened impatiently," Well, this talk about fast advancing technology reminds me how we used to struggle for hours for ensuring faultless typed copies of our dictations to our stenographers in our offices until our manual typewriters were first replaced by electronic typewriters and later with computers with provision to delete, cut and paste. Now with this revolutionary change printing and publishing of not only newspapers and magazines but even of volumes of books have become easy and smooth and, of course, time saving."

Jagan Babu remarked irritably, "Well, I think I have been taken amiss. I simply talked about taming the tiger technology. I did not say that we could do without it."

But Sudhir reacted with a difference, "The point made by Jagan Uncle is very important. Technology is a tool, a medium, which is being used by us, the humans. That means we are at fault, not the technology, we the human beings are at fault."

Jagan Babu did not stop at that and rubbed the issue further, "Well, not because it is old or new, but perhaps governed by factors like over commercialization, things in many areas have not changed in the right direction. I remember my grandfather reading English Daily, lying within a mosquito net, with a kerosene lantern kept over a raised table behind his pillow. I was in school then. It was so easy even a few decades ago to pick up news with clear-cut distinction between advertising, editorials, and articles as their allotment to the pages was very well balanced. Today you keep turning pages till you find on the fourth page what used to be called earlier the front page stories in popular English Dailies with rare exceptions, as first three pages are grabbed as advertising space."

Shamsher added with a smile, "Jagan Bhai, what you are saying is hundred percent true. Commercialization has cast its ever-growing shadow on almost every area of our socio-political activity. Money has gained central stage pushing sanity on the back seat. The bane has crept as well in families affecting adversely the glue that used to keep them bound with emotional threads."

"We cannot go back to the same state of the past," said Goyal. "It is not at all necessary to do so also. But it is equally true that, as we move ahead, lot of aberrations creep in and it is for powers that be to ensure that required steps are taken to keep the system clean from these creeping aberrations."

"Very well said Goyal," said Jagan Babu, "it is for regulators to ensure that the sanctity and fairness is not defiled."

"But that regulators can do things effectively is doubtful," said Shamsher in a tone of utter helplessness.

"Why, Papa?" Narendra could not bear the depressing statement coming from his father who was known for his sanguine optimism.

There was call for the lunch. Even while moving towards dining table, they kept talking.

Shamsher responded to Narendra's query, "You see, it is the man ultimately. And amongst men, while there have been great scientists, writers, philosophers, administrators, there has not been any dearth of merciless villains at all levels whose tales of vicious behaviour, cruelties and brutalities would beat even the most ferocious animals of the jungle. Threat comes from them to every sound looking measure."

"Wah, Shamsher. You are at your intellectual best. Well, we started with something else and ended up with something quite different, but cumulatively it all made sense," Jagan Babu laughed off the seriousness of the discussion.

Lunch over, they all prepared to leave. Jagan Babu thanked them for giving him company. While all youngsters touched his feet, Shamsher in his usual humorous tone gave parting one liner, "It doesn't suit you, Jagan, so do not ever try it with us."

"What?" asked Jagan Babu gaping curiously.

"To be formal," replied Shamsher with a smile and they left him laughing heartily.

Back in his room, Jagan Babu stretched his legs on the bed to relax but the discussions held reverberated still on his mind. He felt sad how film making, which was once used as an effective tool to bring about change for the wellbeing of the society, has gradually reduced to become a blatant instrument for minting money. His mind got entangled in thoughts reflecting on the impact of commercialization of electronic media.

Why films alone, the entire powerful audio-visual medium has turned blatantly commercial with scant regard for the adverse impact it is creating amongst people. The telecast of serials on electronic media has changed the life pattern of almost all the families in the country. Most of them are shown on daily basis with all the melodrama, improbabilities and oddities which speak aloud the lacunae in direction in most of the cases, directors being under pressure to keep them stretching. But why blame producers of the serials, if they have the assurance by the telecasting channels that once begun, they can go on till eternity. As long as they can earn money for the channel, why should they bother about the hapless captive innocent audience, the sentimental lot. But even those blessed with capacity to bear the trash switch off the television the moment there is tragic turn to a story, say the death of a character, because that creates an illusion of the tragedy overtaking almost every household, throwing a wet blanket of grief and depression on all family viewers. This apart, while dramatic situations are successfully created by pitting the helpless innocent characters against the vicious persons, sense of balance is totally missing in almost all serials in the portrayal of good and bad. The villainy is shown at an unbelievable level and proportion while protagonists of the same spectrum representing goodness are portrayed so feeble, unintelligent, and dumb that they are unable to pick even the obvious and naturally time and again keep failing in countering the villainous mechanizations. They look just idiots. Many serials either go off the screen without any logical conclusion or wound up so abruptly that the viewers keep rubbing their palms in utter frustration. In fact, when a serial is allowed to be telecast by a channel as long as the world lasts, the producers have no option but to invent all the gimmicks available to keep it going. Channels, perhaps, look it from different angle. So long as they have got a strong TRP they find it commercially viable to keep them screening whatever happens to the people.

★ ★ ★

LIGHTS AND COLOURS

It was the morning of March 2019. Jagan Babu, who has been witness to now over sixty rounds of all the annual festivals, from brightening lamps of Diwali to colourful frenzy of Holi, stood at the balcony of his flat in New Delhi, watching the sun spreading lazily its shinning rays through the deserted lanes of the colony which, in another couple of hours, began to show signs of colourful day of Holi festival. As he frequented balcony, he watched the slow pace of rising tempo with groups of children throwing tiny water filled balloons on whosoever came in their sight from roads and lanes to the roof tops and balconies of the colony. While fun and frolics amongst children kept rising with rising sun, the youngsters in the family slipped out to join their own groups and families in groups came out and began to visit neighbours in their flats to rub dry colourful powder called Gulal on the faces with exchange of greetings and left to visit others in the colony after tasting Gujiya, the symbolic Holi sweetmeat and some special preparations offered by the host family. When turn of the families came to visit Jagan Babu's flat, the entire family, after having played host, joined the block congregation, and became part of celebrations. After some time, while Ravindra and Ratna continued moving around with neighbouring families, Jagan Babu and Pushpa Devi withdrew to their flat. Rakhi, Pinki, and Rohan had already gone their own ways to enjoy the colours of the festival.

On return, while Pushpa Devi got busy in preparing some traditional dishes, Jagan Babu drew a chair and settled at balcony watching game of colourful hide and seek at different flat compounds. He could not help being nostalgic and recalled his brush with colours of Holi in his growing years.

He recalled how he travelled every year braving the rush of people stacked like bales of cotton in the general compartment of the only late evening train that would carry him to his hometown, Bareilly in Uttar Pradesh. With bubbling energy of the youth, single as a bachelor he could keep struggling throughout the night till the train touched the destination early in the morning and, even at that early hour of five to six, he could not reach home in rickshaw from railway station without being fully drenched in waters of all shades from pleasantly colourful to deep stinking muddy stuff. This was a yearly ritual, until he got married, as reservation in trains during festival times was impossible to be obtained and, come what may, urge to celebrate Holi with the family at home was difficult to be resisted. Even after marriage the ritual of visiting home could continue for a couple of years, but once Pushpa stayed in Delhi, visit to Bareilly was not that feasible. The enthusiasm and tempo of celebrations of Holi at Delhi was nowhere near what he had seen and enjoyed at his hometown. He missed particularly the hub at Baljati Well, which was though a mere well, but had gained the reputation of being monumental and unique because of its make, size, surrounding and ambience. Above all, it was a focal point of learning for the residents of the locality through informal sessions of debates and discussions. He remembered its huge circumference in the middle of large platform which, on the side of a running road, had massive dug up pucca spaces for storing coloured water during Holi festival. The days spent on Holi, year after year till he left Bareilly to join Government service at Delhi, came alive before his eyes. On the day of Holi, male members of the Mohalla would gather in the morning at the space on the side of the triangular road near the platform of Baljati Well, create a bonfire of heap of logs gathered there, which would burn into flames with entire gathering moving around it, chanting slogans in chorus. The robust lots among the gathering would vie with each displaying their lung power through reciting 'Holi Hai' by competitively holding and stretching their breaths. The loud recitations befitting the Holi festival soon used to become a lively loud sport that filled the air with collective energy. This was how ritual of 'Holika Dahan" was collectively celebrated by the residents of the Mohalla. And then would begin the game of throwing colours and rubbing Gulal which transformed everyone into a non-

recognizable species. While throwing of colours, dry and wet, at each other used to continue, the whole lot prepared itself for the dramatic event which was to follow called 'Morcha', the battle of colour. From the huge well on the platform, buckets of water were drawn to fill the deep pits created for storing colourful water and even simple water. The huge water pumps were pushed into the waters of the pits and then there would be noisy wait for attacking parties who came from the adjoining locality equipped with preparation for the battle, with water pumps, and manpower on bullock carts, serving on way cool thandai of Bhang, an intoxicant, massively consumed during Holi by many of the households. As the attacking parties showed up at a distance, the Baljati warriors got ready to confront them with water weapons to force them to quit their territory as losers. And then began actual Morcha, attack and counterattack in one stretch by both sides, with sharp and cutting-edge water fired through huge water pumps. As the tempo of sharp crossfire began to pick up to test the level of tolerance to withstand the attack, he, with his teenager friends, would watch from a corner the crescendo of parties on bullock cart falling and finally dropping down to zero. Now the intruders were on the run to next location for their attack. When Baljati parties gave up, the opposite parties moved on as victors, joined by some of the warriors from Baljati party, who could be accommodated in a friendly gesture. This was the activity at Holi Dahan site which continued till the parties on carts left the mohalla around 11 a.m. and we would return our homes where continued simultaneously rituals with ladies visiting collectively every house in the clusters of our residential complex followed by Rangpashi. That was when we, the zealous lot, would join the fun of throwing coloured water or even simple water to drench others resulting in fast hide and seek game in an endeavour to escape from being caught by the attacking person. Having played the game to the hilt, we the young lot in our notorious twenties, would walk out to join the gangs of friends in the community only to return intoxicated after having consumed unrestricted quantity of bhang thandai.

Lost deep in his thoughts, he was suddenly brought back from the reverie by his grandchildren who had stealthily entered through the half-shut doors of the house and surprised their grandfather in their weird attires. They were forced to change to another round of Holi clothes which they did promptly and now sat there giving company to Jagan Babu who was watching the scene of the lanes in the colony. It was just then that Ravindra and Ratna landed there with dry colours on their faces and took to their seats. Jagan Babu looked at them thoughtfully and prepared himself to meet their queries.

"Dadu, you promised number of times to relate how was Holi celebrated in your teenager. But, somehow, it could not go beyond your struggle in the passenger train to reach Bareilly after you joined service in Delhi," said Pinky stubbornly. Rakhi and Rohan made no less noise to build pressure on him.

"Alright!" Jagan Babu said. "Bachchon, your dadu and papa, as boys, were part of a huge joint family, with close relatives residing in clusters of a huge residential complex in a haphazardly laid Mohalla, symbolized broadly by a monumental structure in the centre of the locality called 'Baljati Well'. The day of Holi used to begin with community function at Baljati Well. I think Ravindra can describe Holika Dahan with graphic details later.

Ravindra who had grown from a child to youth witnessing the scenes as part of them, elaborated, "What Babuji has explained is the common ritual followed everywhere as Holika Dahan, not with the same flavour and fervour as in our mohalla. It was because while everywhere else Holika Dahan is held a day before in the evening, in our mohalla it has traditionally been held in the morning of Rangpashi Day. But what added spice to the ritual was that from that point of Holika Dahan the fun-game of Rangpashi would begin and pick up as the sun would gradually rise higher."

Jagan Babu added with a smile, "Something that I did not see anywhere except in Baljati well function was the game of 'Morcha'. You see when water was being crossfire from water pumps, I just put forward my hand to have the feel of water. Will you believe me I felt the back of my hand being cut by a sharp-edged weapon. I quickly withdrew my hand. And look, they had the force of sharp water on their faces for as long as the battle between two warring parties lasted for a few minutes."

"Very interesting, dadu," Pinky said before others could react.

But Ratna quickly reminded, "Babuji, you promised to relate us……" And before she could complete the sentence, Jagan babu assured her with a gesture, "I remember, Ratna."

"What was that, dadu?" prompted Rohan.

"Well, on one of such day of Rangpashi, I returned home with two of my cousins and two friends with unrecognizable faces, drowned in bhang thandai and we were so hungry that, without bothering to pick plates and saucers, pounced at the eating material, meat, fish, vegetable potato, *dahibade*, *puries* and *kachauries* leaving not a morsel of cooked up food in the kitchen, rubbed hands off with wet tattered clothes on our bodies, went upstairs and fell asleep instantly snoring aloud. The entire family was out at that time visiting neighbouring houses as part of tradition to join them to celebrate Holi and had no inkling of what was happening at our home. I was woken up from deep slumber and brought to senses by persistent shouts and goading of my uncle and was made to learn with foggy mind that the whole house was writhing with anger and ladies cooking passable meals for dozens of hungry stomachs with their tired hands. With red eyes I gazed at my uncle and preferred to pretend not to be in senses to escape his wrath. By evening, friends sneaked out silently and we prepared for our dressing down," Jagan Babu heaved a sigh.

"Nothing of this kind we can imagine to do at all," said Rohan innocently.

As the sun rose high, the roads and lanes became deserted with wet spots here and there visible as marks of intense colourful activities for couple of hours. Not a shadow now was seen on the balconies and compounds of the flats which, a few minutes ago, were alive to the colourful battles within their families. Jagan Babu and others withdrew from the balcony one by one and moved towards bathroom for rubbing off the colours. Hungry like wolves, they pounced at the meals and having finished their lunch they went back with Ravindra, Ratna and Pushpaji to have the story completed. Jagan Babu who had taken couple of stuffed small loaves called *kachories*, cold and solo, his fond breakfast on Holi day, and enjoyed other special festival items like *Gujya* in between, skipped lunch and went back to relax in his bedroom and in no time was caught by nostalgia again.

In Delhi, he recalled, residential colonies warming up to celebrate Holi as a ritual quite late in the day and wound up quite early. He felt sad that while he considered Holi and Diwali as the life blood of our social life and a powerful source of bonding between people of all age groups throughout the whole country, the level of enthusiasm for playfulness associated with Holi has now been scaling down year after year. He imagined a peep down from one corner to other end of India from a low flying aircraft at the peak of celebrations of Holi and Diwali to witness mindboggling sights of colour and light respectively throughout the length and breadth of the country. Now, he lamented, Holi colours seem to be fading year after year because of paucity of time. Earlier, there used to be holidays for a few days preceding the day of Holi which continued for couple of days more and game of throwing colours on people on roads and mohallas began much before the commencement of the actual festival day. In some places like Kanpur and Varanasi in Uttar Pradesh Holi continued to be celebrated for over a week following festival day. He thanked God that Diwali being the festival for worship of Lakshmi, the Goddess of wealth, people's traditional enthusiasm for celebrating the festival with gusto remains intact. The entire market celebrates it investing huge amounts as it involves worship of the Goddess of wealth. He remembered with fondness that before onset of television in the country, Diwali was preceded by Ram Leelas by theatrical parties in colonies and mohallas, every evening till late night, depicting progressively on daily basis the life of lord Ram starting from birth till his return from exile. For a fleeting moment Jagan Babu found himself sitting as a teenager amongst the vast audience to the Ram Leela across the ground near temple in his mohalla on late evenings before Dussehra and even thereafter and he used to laugh with his friends at the boys playing the role of female characters. He used to visit with his family members the site of Dussehra which was celebrated by burning effigies of Ravan and his brothers before huge gatherings, symbolising victory of good over evil. However, with television presenting programmes suitable to the occasions, traditional field performances of Ram Leela have been reduced to almost nil in urban areas. Ram Leelas are, however, performed in rural and semi urban areas even now though not with the same enthusiasm as earlier.

In the evening while sipping tea, Ravindra spoke thoughtfully, "The last ritual of Holi festival fascinated me a lot as a growing child."

"What was that?" asked Rakhi Soberly.

"In the evening, after we had changed to new clothes, all the families would come out and start gathering at the first house at the one end of the mohalla where they were received by the host family and served with special preparations in addition to traditional *gujiya* and *samosas*. Then the entire community, males and children, would visit one house after the other, each house displaying hospitality by offering items prepared as its speciality till the community visited the last house at the end. Tired and over fed we would call it a day and return our homes. That was the close of celebrations of the colourful festival." Ravindra said.

Engrossed in talks, they had no count of time that passed but their gossiping continued.

MULLING IN A MALL

Standing at a considerable height at the Mall in Noida, Jagan Babu was looking down and around and wondered at the magnificence of the modern shopping centre. Though visit to Mall was nothing new for him since he got familiarized with its concept during his visit abroad, he was now at the mall in Delhi after a long time compelled by his fond grandchildren. Rakhi, Rohan and Pinki had walked towards drawing room where Jagan Babu was sitting as usual on his long chair shuffling pages of newspaper.

"Dadu," spoke Pinki loudly to attract the attention of Jagan Babu.

Jagan Babu looked up with question mark on his face folding the newspaper back and putting it aside.

"Dadu! today is Sunday. Papa and mammy have planned to go to Mall of India at Noida this afternoon for some overdue purchases. All of us will be going because we have also to make purchases for ourselves. Dadu, why don't you come with us?"

Jagan Babu did not respond instantly. He was the one who could never enjoy shopping at all. In fact, he visited even local markets only for urgent purchases. Even when he had to go a few years back to famous markets of Delhi like Chandni Chowk, Karol Bagh or Connaught place for shopping for marriages, he only obliged his wife by accompanying her who would do shopping alongwith her daughter or with her close friends and he would sneak out and waited indifferently at some remote corner. He knew how much Pushpa Devi was fond of shopping and loved doing window shopping for hours, something that always irritated Jagan Babu.

After a thoughtful pause he said, "what will I do there? All of you go and enjoy."

"No, dadu! That is not done," Pinki said authoritatively. "You have to come today for our sake."

Ravindra and Ratna who were hearing the conversation, came out of the bedroom and pleaded with Jagan Babu to agree to accompany them. And Jagan Babu had to give up. It was decided that Rakhi, Rohan and Pinki would go by metro or cab and all others in the family would accompany Ravindra in his car.

And now at the mall while all others in the family were hopping from one shop to the other, he stood at some vantage point watching people moving from one level to the other on escalators.

Having spent some time standing and watching the glamourous setting, he retreated to a corner of the shopping area to relax and as soon as he found the place to sit, he settled down and, stirred by the ambience of mall, he was overtaken by nostalgic flash back.

He found himself seated in an aeroplane that took him in 1996 across the sea to advanced western countries where he sojourned for over a fortnight and every place that he visited had offered him something new to ponder upon. In Miami, he had the experience of travelling for the first time on Metro rail, something which was nowhere in sight then in India except that modest beginning had been made in Calcutta, but its tardy progress did not evoke any hope for future of metro in India. It was then only a dream. But now it is a feast to his eyes when metros are seen in Delhi moving over the ground, under the ground and on elevated corridors. Now to him, massive use of metro's expanding network in Delhi and other cities of India is a game changer since it not only caters to around twenty five lakhs daily riders in Delhi alone but also because it provides a natural training ground for people to exercise restraint, to keep patience and to conduct themselves with discipline as against earlier torturous long unmanaged queues and painful bus-trips with passengers stuffed as bales of cotton and lot many hanging precariously at the doors. It was again in Miami that he witnessed for the first-time prevailing sense of respect for pedestrians. He, with his colleagues, stood on one side to cross the road and, speeding cars began to stop at their own, one by one, until they crossed the road. Later he came across, for the first time, a pedestrian crossing signal. People in metropolitans in India are now learning to use pedestrian tracks created for them. He recalled how desperately he looked for a place where he could throw the cigarette butt after he finished enjoying puffs while sitting at Bay Side. He found that all round sense of cleanliness was a perpetual treat to his eyes during his two week's sojourns to Port of Spain, the capital of Trinidad and Tobago, to United States and then to some of the European countries. He thought with a sense of relief that, even though slowly, people in India have been endeavouring to imbibe the precious virtue of cleanliness.

"Dadu, will you like to have tea or coffee?" enquired Rakhi emerging from one of the nearby counters.

Jagan Babu returned to the present with a slight jerk and said, "No! Rakhi. I took tea at home and that was good enough for me."

As Rakhi went back to the nearby shop, Jagan Babu again slipped into his past.

He recalled how he had felt depressed when he could not make it to accompany advance official team to Trinidad & Tobago and missed to visit London in transit, the place he craved most for sojourn since his childhood. He had always desired to see the country whose sun did never set as also to understand how handful of people could keep under their control big colonies like India for over two centuries despite winds blew fast and ferocious against their tyrannous rule. He was keen to see the places to which his fond English writers and poets belonged. But fate, perhaps, had decided to compensate him with far more generous a deal than the one he bemoaned as having missed. In a couple of years' time, he was picked up for an assignment and stayed in London for a whole fortnight with all required facilities. Then he did not merely smell the town but felt it also from close corners. He was intrigued by the illusion of invisibility of Police personnel who would appear like ghosts from nowhere at the spot on slightest provocations. Then, he was over awed by the august complex of the then most famous mall of the world, Harrods. There he could for the first time watch, when he walked at its different levels, the magnificence, magnitude, and multiplicity of shopping divisions within a complex. Later, though he walked in many malls and saw gradually changing pattern of shopping culture in India, it was in a small shopping centre in Dubai where he could see for the first time vegetables cleanly wrapped, catalogued and categorized, fish and chicken cut into pieces and kept in wrap in different weights, all items ready to be picked by customers. And, despite all this sophistication, he missed traditional vegetable markets of his hometown where he would go with a bag from one zig-zag lane to the other amidst loud selling voices of vegetable sellers, with dozens of green fresh varieties kept in heaps before each of them. The entire market resounded with cacophony of voices of customers higgling and haggling and vendors shouting to invite attention of the customers. He could also not help recalling the atmosphere surcharged with loudness typical of vegetable markets and would bargain on and on till the big bag was ready to burst. There used to be fish market adjacent to vegetable market where varieties of living fish were kept protected in water tubs to be picked up by customer. Chicken was a rarity then as poultry was only a small home industry. But there were mutton shops in markets of the mohallas with set family customers, who normally tried to trust the butchers though generally they found it difficult to rely on them as a class.

"Dadu, mammy and papa are waiting for you in Men's Section," Rohan spoke aloud as he found Jagan Babu dozing.

Hearing Rohan's voice Jagan Babu reverted back from nostalgia and found Pinki and Rohan loaded with bags in their hands. He accompanied them silently and when asked to select shirts and Pants for himself he declined saying that he had enough, and that otherwise also readymade stuff did not fit in properly on his body. But he could not resist any longer the affectionate persuasions of his children and agreed to select the articles which suited him.

While others kept looking for different articles for purchase, Jagan Babu came back again to the space where he was sitting and found a boy occupying part of the space. As he came to sit there the boy created space for him. He sat down and watched for some time people passing with bags in their hands. The boy was reading a book. As he looked towards Jagan Babu, he asked the boy about his education and was told that he was tenth class student. Probed further, the boy told him that he would be trying for medical.

Ravindra, Ratna and Pushpa Devi came finally at the spot where Jagan Babu was sitting and waited for Rakhi, Rohan and Pinki to join them before they thought of disturbing Jagan Babu who they found as usual lost in thoughts. After a little while when Jagan Babu lifted eyes and saw them standing, he welcomed them with sarcastic smile, "So, the shopping is over at last. What next?"

Pinki responded spontaneously, "Food Court, dadu."

"Okay! As you say. Let us go then," said Jagan Babu and they all moved.

They reached Food Court, a huge section with different food stalls, from north-Indian vegetarian and non-vegetarian preparations to South-Indian dosas and *idli*, from Chinese Chow Mein, Noodles, Hot Pot to Italian Pasta, Risotto and Gnocchi. They occupied tables and settled on comfortable chairs. All of them picked up the food of their choice and brought on the table for Jagan Babu and Pushpa Devi after consulting them.

It was not for the first time that Jagan Babu was taking meals at a mall. But every time he ate at a mall, he could not help recalling various hotels like 'Kake di Hatti' of Connaught Place, the eating stalls at Chandni Chawk and even remembering his student days when he and his friends, would quite frequently go to Frontier Hotel outside the railway station when chicken was considered to be a rarity. For a change they would take *Kachouri Aloo* at Manga and Panna, who were famous for the recipe in the entire town.

"Dadu, how do you like the food here?" asked Rohan picking up chow Mein from the fork.

"Very nice," replied Jagan Babu who was enjoying *Chholey Bhaturay*. He knew that he was trying to drag him to a discussion involving unavoidable comparisons with food outlets now and then during his days in college.

"Dadu, I am sure that after your visits to various malls in India and abroad, you must have appreciated the concept of mall that has revolutionized the whole marketing pattern," said Rakhi to elicit Jagan Babu's reaction. "In India, though traditional markets exist still attracting customers in huge numbers, the fact that most of things required are available at one place with ambience soothing to the eyes has made malls not only the place easier for the people to make buying pleasant and easier, but people find them suitable for periodic visits for change from the monotonous daily routine. Opening of multiplex in malls, which have caused most of the single screen theatres to close down, is an added benefit for visitors who can see film after proper selection. Wouldn't you agree, dadu, that life has wonderfully changed for the better."

Jagan Babu heard Rakhi with supressed smile as he knew that she was making a case for "all- too- good in modern world'. He kept silent for some moments giving the impression that he agreed fully with her. And he really agreed with her to a great extent. But, with experience of seven decades behind him, it was not easy for him to agree fully with Rakhi.

"You are right Rakhi. But I would like to add something to complete the picture. At eatery sector, big, branded chains like Haldiram, Bikanervala have practically captured the whole traditional market. Facilities like 'home delivery' and 'Take Away' have also made tremendous difference. However, it can be noted with some satisfaction that traditional outlets and old market practices have been successfully trying to coexist taking innovative steps of their own. Otherwise, it is the same old game of big and small fish. But we cannot put the clock back."

Rakhi, Rohan and Pinki had not expected Jagan Babu to agree with Rakhi so conveniently who had eulogized concept of mall as a symbol of change which has made life better than before. They expected him to dig holes in the concept of expanding phenomenon of malls which were mushrooming now in different sizes. But they missed to read between the lines when he talked of coexistence of traditional markets and big and small fish game.

Dinner over, Jagan Babu accompanied by Pushpa and Ratna moved to underground parking lot and were on their way back home in the car driven by Ravindra. Rohan, Rakhi and Pinki took a cab from outside the mall. Back home, everyone got involved in activities from hearing music to study in their bedrooms.

Jagan Babu settled down in his long side chair in his study room. Stirred by the grandeur of malls which he has been visiting in India and abroad in recent years, he got engrossed in nostalgia closing gradually his thoughtful eyes.

Despite spread of colourful malls and similar other outfits, he could not help getting lost recalling the colourfulness that surpassed all that he has seen so far, the rare feeling of colourful dream conjuring the ambience of Brindavan Garden in Mysore of early seventies when he, with his family, had landed there with evening lights on. It was a mesmerizing site to watch while walking the distance of miles in the garden side by side with soothing multi-coloured water with an aura of celestial bliss spread all over the place. The impact was so powerful that he could not resist the wish to revisit the site in Mysore when he went on tour to Bangalore after three decades. Having reached Mysore filled with silent expectation after around three hours of travel by road, it was the worst disappointment that he ever had in the past. The lights were on, but it was the most lack-lustre walk towards the garden, which, in order to accommodate water pipes as part of development activity, was shifted a few miles ahead. When he expressed surprise at the changed scenario, he was told by accompanying colleague that it was the cost of development that we had to pay. He agreed with him recalling the visit of his family accompanied by one of his friends family to Badrinath shrine recently. As their taxi entered the township of Badrinath, he was aghast to see the scenario akin to the heart of a crowded place of pilgrimage like Rishikesh which, while to first timers did not make any difference, but turned out to be a disillusionment to him as one who had visited the place earlier four decades ago. Accompanied by his colleagues, he had landed on jeep at Badrinath near the temple and was enthralled, on one hand, by the aura of piety engulfing the area, and, on the other, fascinated by natural beauty surrounding the area with patches of snow dotted all over the ground a few yards away from the temple. The flowing water of the river across the temple added beauty to the area and three springs of hot, tepid and cold water, called kunds, which now lay eclipsed by the multitudes of bathing lot, existed there facing the temple for dips by the faithfuls. Visitors to the place could be counted on fingers. They enjoyed the dips, did puja and had memorable adventure on way back to Joshimath as the darkness of the evening began to grow thick. The road had collapsed leading to very long queue of stranded vehicles. He and his accompanying colleagues had to spend the night at the army camp in the fragile light of candles, courtesy camp bosses who recognized their contribution as media persons.

He did not know when he fell asleep. He awoke at some noise only to vaguely remember the crux of his nostalgic flashback which reverberated in his mind like beat of a hammer that change doesn't come without exacting some cost.

★ ★ ★

In the evening while Ravindra was busy in repairing some electrical kitchen gadget and Ratna was in and out the kitchen as usual, Rakhi, followed by Rohan and Pinki, came in the drawing room and looked at Jagan Babu silently watching usual cock fight called debate on the television.

As soon as Jagan Babu looked towards his grandchildren, Rakhi asked him, "Dadu, like films, television is also audio-visual medium. Is it as powerful a medium as films?"

"Yes Rakhi. But both have their distinct formatting and traits which distinguish one from the other. Television is now household name and people, mostly housewives, view serials, films and different programmes of their liking. What started in 1959 as an experimental telecast with makeshift studio has developed gradually to be the most powerful wing of Indian media."

"When did you first purchase a television set, Dadu?" asked Rohan.

"In the beginning I purchased a black and white television because coloured television came in the market much later. Your papa and uncles and buas were just growing children when they watched with us the programmes alongwith children and adults of neighbourhoods who would gather at our house to see weekly films programme and popular serials telecast on Doordarshan then. Subsequently another channel was introduced besides adding channels to provide regional coverage through their respective languages. For long it needed a huge antenna to be fixed at the roof tops," explained Jagan Babu.

Before he could proceed further Ravindra cried aloud, "Yes, one of us would be shouting from the top of the roof adjusting the direction of antenna while display at the screen was being monitored with exchange of shouts. Everyone in the locality knew that antenna was being adjusted. How funny was it. But we enjoyed it."

"Then later coloured television came to replace black and white," continued Jagan Babu in the same vein. "Thereafter it is the story of fast growth and expansion of television. And now, as you see, television has come to occupy central stage with number of private channels added up. The long metal antenna was replaced gradually by cable wires and also came up various other relaying channels. In fact, Dish T.V, which launched the first Direct Broadcast satellite service, popularly called DTH service, in October 2003 has changed the face of Indian Television by making it possible for every customer to access its contents. If I remember correctly there are now six DTH providers, Airtel Digital TV; Dish TV; Sun Direct; Reliance Digital TV; Videocon d2h and Tata Sky.

"Dadu, how was it when you and *chotey dadus* were in schools and colleges?" Rohan enjoyed stories relating to dadu's boyhood days.

"Well, in our college days, the only source of entertainment for us was going to a film in a theatre. As was in most of the towns, there were four to five theatres in Bareilly namely Jagat, Novelty, Hind, Kumar, Kamal, and we, the boys, would go to watch films stealthily dodging our families.," Jagan Babu explained. "However, for families it was a formidable task and for months they would not be able to go to a film theatre. And now, with remote in your hand, you can surf the film of your choice on popular channels and films produced on OTT film Platforms including Netflix, Disney & hotstar, Amazon Prime, Zee5 and Voot. And let us not forget that it is one of the biggest source of learning and acquiring knowledge, from wildlife to human rights. It depends on us how we use it."

Dinner was ready, they were called on the dining table. They kept talking slowly while serving the eatables in their plates. After dinner they withdrew to their bedrooms.

★ ★ ★

EPILOGUE

The story of 'unstoppable change' can go on and on beyond the limited space of these sheets, change which is perceptibly gratifying pervading across the whole of India. Having breathed the fresh air of freedom, psyche of abject servility has gone and we now stand up to hold our position with dignity unmindful of our station in life. Even the poorest of poor amongst us feel no longer harassed by the horn of a magnificent car.

In the decade of fifties, feasts in marriages were served on pattals (leaf-plates) baked clay saucers and mud-cups and the left over used to be dumped outside only to be pounced at by starving families of the area. Poor are fed by the rich even now, but they take it with dignity and left-over they seldom relish. The class of scavengers has practically vanished.

In the decade 1950s, if a poor worker, a rickshaw puller or a labourer, was being thrashed mercilessly by a dying shadow of feudalistic lord for a minor fault, people would watch from the distance, but none had the guts to intervene. Now you touch him and you will have it to your neck by the gathered crowd of his clan before you discover what has happened to you.

A policeman in khaki uniform used to be terror in a locality during the years immediately after attainment of Independence. Fear of khaki as a symbol of terror has gradually been replaced by courage and strength to stand up against injustice.

While the gap between rich and poor inevitably exists, the gap in terms of untouchability has narrowed down considerably with evolving social ethos where each one ventures to have a place of dignity. We are now aware of our rights and are conscious to protect them at all costs. And that is SumTotal of the change that has occurred in India in preceding seven decades.

And this proves the veracity of pious words once spoken by Lord Buddha: 'If we could see the miracle of a single flower clearly, our whole life would change'.

www.ingramcontent.com/pod-product-compliance
Lightning Source LLC
Chambersburg PA
CBHW021215130726
47988CB00002B/670